Dedalus European Classics
General Editor: Timothy Lane

THE SHORT STORIES OF GUSTAV MEYRINK

VOLUME II (THE MASTER AND OTHER STORIES)

GUSTAV MEYRINK

THE SHORT STORIES OF GUSTAV MEYRINK

VOLUME II (THE MASTER AND OTHER STORIES)

translated by Mike Mitchell

Dedalus

Supported using public funding by
**ARTS COUNCIL
ENGLAND**

Published in the UK by Dedalus Limited
24-26, St Judith's Lane, Sawtry, Cambs, PE28 5XE
email: info@dedalusbooks.com
www.dedalusbooks.com

ISBN printed book 978 1 915568 05 2
ISBN ebook 978 1 915568 37 3

Dedalus is distributed in the USA & Canada by SCB Distributors
15608 South New Century Drive, Gardena, CA 90248
info@scbdistributors.com   www.scbdistributors.com

Dedalus is distributed in Australia by Peribo Pty Ltd
58, Beaumont Road, Mount Kuring-gai, N.S.W. 2080
info@peribo.com.au   www.peribo.com.au

First published in Germany in 1913
First published by Dedalus in 2023
Translation of *The Short Stories of Gustav Meyrink Volume II copyright ©
Mike Mitchell 2023*

The right of Mike Mitchell to be identified as the translator of this work has
been asserted by him in accordance with the Copyright, Designs and Patents
Act, 1988.

Printed and bound in the UK by Clays Elcograf S.p.A.
Typeset by Marie Lane

A C.I.P. listing for this book is available on request.

THE TRANSLATOR

MIKE MITCHELL

Mike Mitchell has been a freelance literary translator since 1995. *The Short Stories of Gustav Meyrink Volume II (The Master & Other Stories)* is his ninety-ninth translation from German and French.

His translations include, including Gustav Meyrink's five novels and *The Dedalus Book of Austrian Fantasy.* His translation of Rosendorfer's *Letters Back to Ancient China* won the 1998 Schlegel-Tieck Translation Prize after he had been shortlisted in previous years for his translations of *Stephanie* by Herbert Rosendorfer and *The Golem* by Gustav Meyrink.

His translations have been shortlisted four times for The Oxford Weidenfeld Translation Prize: *Simplicissimus* by Johann Grimmelshausen in 1999, *The Other Side* by Alfred Kubin in 2000, *The Bells of Bruges* by Georges Rodenbach in 2008 and *The Lairds of Cromarty* by Jean-Pierre Ohl in 2013. His biography of Gustav Meyrink: *Vivo: The Life of Gustav Meyrink* was published by Dedalus in November 2008.

CONTENTS

THE MASTER

Leonhard sits in his Gothic chair, motionless, eyes wide, staring into space.

The flames blazing up from the twigs in the small fireplace send the light flickering over his hair shirt, but the immobility surrounding him allows it no purchase, and it slides off his long white beard, his furrowed face and old man's hands so deathly still they seem part of the brown and gold of the arms of the chair.

Leonhard is staring at the window. Outside, the ruinous, half-tumbledown castle chapel where he is sitting is surrounded by snowy mounds the height of a man, but his mind's eye sees the bare, narrow, unadorned walls behind him, the squalid pile of bedding and the crucifix over the worm-eaten door, sees the jug of water, the loaf of bread he baked himself from beechnut flour and next to it the knife with the notched bone handle in the corner recess.

He hears the huge trees crack under the hard frost and

sees, in the harsh, sharp-edged moonlight, the icicles glittering on the branches groaning under their burden of white. He sees his own shadow stretching out through the pointed arch of the window and joining the silhouettes of the fir trees in a spectral dance over the sparkling snow as the flames leap up and down; at other times he sees it shrink to the figure of a goat on a blue-black throne with the knobs on his chair forming a pair of devil's horns above pointed ears.

An old, hunchbacked woman from the kiln, which is down in the valley hours away across the moor, hobbles laboriously through the trees, pulling a sledge loaded with dry wood. Startled, she gapes at the brilliant light, uncomprehending. Her eye falls on the devilish shadow on the snow and she realises where she is, that she is outside the chapel where, according to legend, the last scion of a cursed line, immune to death, lives out his empty life.

Seized with horror, she crosses herself and hurries back into the forest, knees trembling.

In his mind's eye Leonhard follows her for a while along the path. It takes him past the fire-blackened ruins of the castle beneath which his childhood lies buried, but he feels no emotion, for him everything is present, beyond suffering, clear as a shape formed out of coloured air. He sees himself as a child, playing with bright pebbles under a young birch tree, and at the same time he sees himself as an old man sitting watching his shadow.

The figure of his mother appears before him, her features twitching as always. Everything about her is in a constant quiver of restlessness, only the skin on her forehead is unmoving, smooth as parchment and stretched tight over her round skull, like an ivory sphere imprisoning a swarm of thoughts which buzz like flies to get out.

He hears the constant rustle of her black silk dress, never silent for a moment, filling the castle with the exasperating buzz of millions of insects, finding its way through every gap in walls or floorboards, robbing everyone, man and beast alike, of their peace. Those thin lips, ever ready to snap out a command, hold even objects in thrall; they seem to be permanently on the alert, not one of them daring to make itself comfortable. She only knows of what goes on in the world outside from hearsay and thinks that searching for the meaning of life is a waste of time, merely an excuse for idleness. As long as the house is filled from morning till night with pointless, ant-like scurrying around, needless moving of things from here to there, feverish activity to the point of exhaustion and sleep, wearing down everything and everyone, she believes she is fulfilling her duty in life.

No thought ever reaches fruition in her mind. Hardly has one entered her head than it is transformed into hasty, pointless action.

She is like the second hand on a clock, forever jerking forward and imagining, in its insignificance, that the world would come to a standstill if it didn't keep twitching, three thousand six hundred times an hour, twelve hours a day, grinding time to dust and impatiently waiting for the placid hour-hand to give the signal for the bell to chime.

In the middle of the night her obsessive restlessness often drags her from her bed and she wakes the servants: the interminable rows of flower pots on the window ledges must be watered at once. She cannot say why, it is enough that they 'must' be watered. No one dares to gainsay her, everyone is struck dumb, since to reason with her is as hopeless as trying to fight a will-o'-the-wisp with a sword. None of her plants take root as she repots them daily, birds never perch on the castle roof; driven on by a deep-seated instinct they criss-cross the sky, wheeling this way and that, up and down, now appearing as dots, now broadening out into black, fluttering hands. Even the sun's rays are eternally atremble, for there is always a wind hustling the clouds to blot out their light. The leaves and branches are swirled and ruffled from morn till eve and fruits never ripen, the May breezes themselves blow away the blossom. All around, nature is sick from the restlessness in the castle.

Leonhard sees himself, twelve years old, sitting at his sums, pressing his hands hard over his ears so as not to hear the slamming of doors, the constant up-and-down of the maids on the stairs or the shrill of his mother's voice. But it's no use, the numbers turn into a herd of tiny, spiteful, wriggling goblins, run through his brain, through his nose, in and out of his eyes and ears, making his blood boil and his skin burn. He tries reading — in vain, the letters dance before his eyes like a blurry cloud of midges.

'Have you still not done that exercise?' He starts at the sound of his mother's voice, but she doesn't wait for an answer, her watery blue eyes are already flitting from one corner to the next to see if she can spot a trace of dust. Non-existent spider's webs have to be brushed off, pieces of furniture moved, carried out and brought back in again, wardrobes taken apart to make sure there are no moths, table legs are screwed off and on again, drawers fly open and shut, pictures are rehung, nails torn out of the walls and knocked back in one inch away, objects are seized with a frenzy, the hammerhead flies off the shaft, rungs of the ladder break, plaster trickles down the wall — fetch the plasterer at once! — cloths get stuck, needles slip out of hands and hide in gaps in the floorboards, the watchdog in the courtyard breaks loose, comes rushing in, its chain clattering behind it, and knocks over the grandfather clock. Little Leonhard immerses himself in his book again and grits his teeth, trying to get some sense out of the curly black pothooks chasing each other across the page. He must sit somewhere else, the chair has to have the dust beaten out of it. He leans on the window ledge, a book in his hand — the window ledge has to be washed, has to be painted white. Why is he always in the way, and has he finally done that exercise? Then she sweeps out. The maids have to drop everything, quickly, follow her and get shovels, axes and sticks in case there are rats in the cellar.

The window ledge is half painted, the chairs are all minus their seats and the room is a scene of devastation. Dull, unbounded hatred of his mother eats into the boy's heart. With his every fibre he yearns for peace. He longs for night to come, but even sleep does not bring the desired rest, confused dreams split his thoughts in two, chasing but never catching each other. His muscles find it impossible to relax, his whole body is tensed, waiting for a lightning order to do some pointless activity or other.

His daytime games in the garden are not the expression of childish exuberance, his mother decrees them mindlessly, like everything she does, to interrupt them the next moment. To her, persevering with one thing for any length of time looks like inactivity, which she feels she must fight against as she would fight against death. The boy does not dare leave the castle, always stays within earshot. He feels there is no escape; one step too far and a loud command from the open window will shackle his feet.

Little Sabina ia a peasant girl a year younger than Leonhard who lives with the servants. He only ever sees her from a distance, and if they do manage to talk for a few brief moments, they speak in rushed, disjointed phrases, like people on passing ships calling out a few hurried words to each other.

The old count, Leonhard's father, is lame in both legs. He spends all day in a wheelchair in his library, always just about to start reading, but even there he has no peace. At regular intervals Leonhard's mother appears and her restless fingers root around in the books, dust them and clap them together, sending markers fluttering to the floor. Volumes which are here today are on the top shelf tomorrow, or piled up in mountains on the floor if the wallpaper behind suddenly has to be brushed or rubbed down with slices of bread. Even when the Countess is occupied in other rooms, that only increases the mental confusion and torment of the nagging suspense that any moment she might unexpectedly reappear.

In the evening, when the candles are lit, little Leonhard creeps in to be with his father, to keep him company, but they never talk. It is as if there were a glass wall between them, making understanding impossible. Sometimes the old man excitedly leans forward and opens his mouth, as if he had suddenly made up his mind to tell his son something important, something with far-reaching consequences, but the words always stick in his throat, he closes his lips and just mutely, tenderly strokes the boy's burning forehead, and even as he does so his gaze flickers towards the door through which interruption might come at any moment.

The boy has a vague sense of what is going on inside his father, that it is the fullness, not the emptiness of his heart that ties his tongue. Once again, he feels the bitter hatred of his mother rise in his gorge. In his mind he perceives an obscure connection between her and the deep furrows and distraught expression on the old man's face in the cushions of the wheelchair. A wish that his mother might be found dead in her bed one morning quietly surfaces inside him, adding the agony of waiting to the constant torment of inner unrest. Secretly he observes her features in the mirror, looking for any trace of illness, watches her as she walks, hoping to discover the signs of incipient debility. But the woman remains as fit as a fiddle, never shows the slightest weakness, indeed, seems to draw new strength the more the people around her grow jaded and infirm.

From Sabina and the servants Leonhard learns that his father is a philosopher, a wise man, and that all the books are full of wisdom, so he resolves, in his childish fashion, to acquire wisdom. Perhaps then the invisible barrier separating him from his father will fall, the furrowed brow be smoothed, the bitter old man's face young again. But no one can tell him what wisdom is. He turns to the priest, but his orotund, 'The fear of the Lord is the beginning of wisdom,' only succeeds in confusing him more.

One thing he is absolutely convinced of is that his mother does *not* know, and it slowly begins to dawn on him that everything she thinks and does must be the opposite of wisdom.

One evening when they are alone together for a moment, he plucks up his courage, and abruptly, haltingly, like someone crying out for help, asks his father what wisdom is. He sees the muscles in his father's clean-shaven face straining with the effort of finding the right words for the mind of an inquiring child. His own head is almost bursting with the effort of trying to understand what his father is saying. He realises why the sentences coming from the toothless mouth are so hurried, so fragmentary. It is his father's fear of interruption by his mother, his concern lest the sacred seeds be corrupted by the corrosive matter-of-fact aura she exudes. If Leonhard should misunderstand them, they could easily send up poisonous shoots.

All his endeavours to understand are in vain. Already he can hear the loud footsteps bustling along the corridor, the curt, shrill commands and the terrible rustling of her black silk dress. His father speaks faster and faster. He tries to catch his words, to store them up so he can think about them later, grabbing at them as if they were knives whistling through the air, but they slip from his grasp, leaving bloody cuts.

The breathless utterances: 'the longing for wisdom itself is wisdom' — 'search for a fixed point within yourself, my child, that the world cannot reach' — 'regard everything that happens as a lifeless painting and do not let yourself be touched by it', pierce his heart, but it is as if they were wearing masks he cannot penetrate. He is about to ask another question, but the door is already flying open. One last piece of advice — 'let time run off you like water' — floats past his ear, then the Countess rushes in, a bucket topples over on the threshold, a flood of dirty water pours over the tiles. 'Don't get in the way!

Make yourself useful!' The words echo behind him as, filled with despair, he dashes down the stairs to his room.

The images of childhood fade and once more Leonhard is looking at the white forest in the moonlight outside his chapel window and it is no clearer, nor fainter than the scenes from the days of his youth. To the adamantine clarity of his mind reality and memory are equally lifeless and alive.

A fox trots past, lean-limbed, silent. The snow spouts up in a glittering puff where its bushy tail touches the ground, its eyes glow green in the darkness of the trunks, then disappear in the undergrowth.

In his mind's eye Leonhard sees scrawny figures in shabby clothes, vacant, expressionless faces, different in age and yet so strangely similar, hears names whispered in his ear, unmemorable, everyday names, which scarcely serve to distinguish their bearers. In them he recognises his tutors, who come and then go after a month. His mother is never satisfied with them, dismisses them one after the other without knowing nor asking herself the reason. All that matters is that they are there and then gone again, like bubbles in seething waters.

Leonhard is a youth with down on his lip and already as tall as his mother. When he stands facing her, his eyes are on the same level as hers, but he always feels compelled to look away, not daring to give way to the constant prick of the urge to fix her vacant stare and pour into it all the searing hatred he feels for her. Each time he chokes it back and the saliva in his mouth tastes bitter as gall, his blood feels poisoned.

He pries and probes within himself, but cannot find what makes him so powerless in the face of this woman with her restless, bat-like zigzag flight. A chaos of ideas is swirling round inside his head like a wheel spinning out of control, each heartbeat washes another scum of half-grasped thoughts into his mind and washes it away again. Jostling and shattering against each other, plans that are no such thing, contradictory ideas, aimless desires, blind, ravenous cravings emerge from the turbulence of the depths, which immediately suck them back in again. Screams suffocate in his breast, unable to reach the surface.

Leonhard is in the grip of a wild, howling despair which grows stronger with each day. His mother's detested face haunts him. A ghostly apparition, it stares out from every corner, leaps up at him from every book he opens. He is incapable of turning the page, for fear of seeing it again, does not dare look round in case it is behind him. Every shadow congeals into the dreaded features, the sound of his own breath is like the rustle of her silk dress.

His senses are as sore and tender as an exposed nerve. When he is in bed, he does not know whether he is dreaming or awake, and when sleep finally does overcome him, her figure rises up from the floor in her nightgown, wakes him and screeches in his ear, 'Leonhard, are you asleep already?'

Now he is convulsed by a new, strangely hot sensation, which constricts his breathing, pursues him and drives him to seek out Sabina, without really knowing what it is he wants from her. She is grown up. Her dresses come down to her ankles and the rustling of her skirt arouses him even more than that of his mother's.

Understanding with his father is impossible now, his mind is completely clouded by madness. At regular intervals the old man's ghastly groans interrupt the hustle and bustle of the house, hour by hour they swab his face with vinegar, push his wheelchair here and there, torture the dying man to death.

Leonhard buries his head in the pillows so as not to hear. A servant plucks at his sleeve. 'Quick, for God's sake come quick, the old Count's almost gone!' Leonhard jumps up, doesn't know where he is, how the sun can be shining, why it isn't deepest night if his father is dying. He staggers, telling himself with numb lips that it is all a dream, then hurries over to the sickroom. Wet towels are hanging up to dry on lines stretched right across the room, baskets block his way, the wind is roaring in through the open windows, making the white linen billow; from somewhere in the corner comes the sound of the death rattle.

Leonhard tears down the clotheslines — wet washing smacks onto the floor — flings everything aside and forces a way through to the wheelchair from which the eyes, as the final curtain falls, fix him with a blind, glassy stare. He collapses to his knees and presses the unresponsive hand, damp with the cold sweat of death, to his forehead. He tries to cry out, 'Father!', but the word will not come, it has suddenly been expunged from his memory. It is on the tip of his tongue, but the next moment, seized with terror, he has forgotten it, choked by a mind-numbing fear that the dying man will never regain his senses if he doesn't call out that word to him. That word alone has the power to call the fading consciousness back over the threshold of life, if only for a brief second. He tears his hair and beats his face. A thousand words bombard him, only the one word, the word he is seeking with all the fervour of his heart, refuses to come, and the death rattle is growing weaker and weaker — halts — starts again — breaks off — for ever.

The jaw drops. The mouth stays open.

'Father!' Leonhard cries. At last, the word has come, but the man to whom it is addressed will never move again.

Uproar on the stairs, screaming voices, running steps echoing up and down the passages; the dog starts barking, interspersed with howls. Leonhard pays no attention, all he can see and feel is the terrible calm on the rigid, lifeless face. It fills the room with a radiance which illumines, envelops him. A dizzying sense of a happiness he has never known lays its hand on his heart, an intimation of an unchanging present beyond past and future, a mute rejoicing in the discovery that all around is the pulsation of a force in which he can take refuge, as if in a cloud that makes him invisible, from the restless maelstrom of the house.

The air is filled with brightness.

Tears are pouring down Leonhard's cheeks.

He starts as the door opens with a clatter. His mother comes tearing in. 'No time for crying now. Can't you see we're rushed off our feet?' Her words cut like a whiplash. The orders come tumbling out, the one countermanded by the next, the maids sob and get thrown out, in frantic haste the servants carry the furniture out into the corridor, panes of glass rattle, medicine bottles smash.

'Get the doctor!... No, no, the priest... stop, stop, not the priest, the gravedigger, tell him not to forget his spade... and to bring a coffin too, with nails to nail it down... and someone go and open up the chapel, prepare the family vault, at once, right away!... And where are those candles that should be burning? And why is no one laying out the corpse? Do you have to be told everything ten times over?!'

With a shudder Leonhard sees how the frenzied witches' sabbath of life does not even pause before the majesty of death and step by step wins a hideous victory. He feels the peace within him vanish like the morning dew.

Slavishly obedient hands are already being laid on the wheelchair to bear the Count away. Leonhard tries to intervene, to protect the dead man. He spreads his arms, but they drop back feebly to his sides. He grits his teeth and forces himself to look his mother in the eye to see if there is the slightest hint of sorrow or grief there, but not for one second can he hold her shifting, restless gaze. Like a monkey's, her eyes are constantly on the move, flitting from corner to corner, up and down, from ceiling to wall, from window to door with the zigzag flight of a demented blowfly, revealing a creature with no soul. Pain and passion bounce off her like arrows off a whirling target, she is a giant insect in the form of a woman, a woman possessed, embodying the curse of aimless, pointless toil on earth. A spurt of dread paralyses Leonhard. He stares at her, horrified, as if she were a creature he were looking at for the first time. There is nothing human about her any longer, she appears to him as an alien being from some hell, half goblin, half vicious animal.

The idea that this is his mother turns his own blood into a noxious substance, eating away at his body and soul. His hair stands on end in a sudden onrush of horror at himself that drives him out — anywhere as long as it is away from her! He rushes into the park with no idea where he is going, what he is doing, crashes into a tree and falls on his back, unconscious.

Leonhard is staring at a new image crossing his inner

vision like a fevered dream: the chapel suffused with candle-light, a priest muttering at the altar, a scent of withering wreaths, an open coffin, the dead Count in his white cloak of office, his waxy yellow hands crossed on his chest. A glint of gold in dark pictures of saints, black-clad men standing in a semi-circle, lips mumbling prayers, cold musty air coming up from the floor and an iron trapdoor with a shining cross propped open: the square, yawning hole leads down into the crypt. Muted chanting in Latin, sunlight coming in through the stained-glass windows, dappling the drifts of incense with patches of green, blue, blood-red, an insistent, silvery ringing from the ceiling, the priest's hand in its lacy sleeve waving the aspergillum over the dead man's face. Suddenly there is movement: twelve white-gloved hands bestir themselves, lift the bier from the catafalque and close the lid; the ropes go taut, the coffin sinks into the depths, the men descend the stone steps. Then a dull echo from the vault, the crunch of sand, solemn stillness. Grave faces emerge silently from the crypt, the trapdoor descends, the lock snaps shut, dust swirls up round the edges, the cross is now horizontal. The candles gutter, go out; once more the light comes from the pine twigs in the fireplace; altar and pictures are replaced by bare walls, the flagstones covered with soil; the wreaths crumble to dust, the figure of the priest dissolves into air. Leonhard is alone again.

Since the death of the old count, the servants' quarters are in turmoil. They refuse to obey the pointless commands, one after the other they pack their things and leave. The few that are left are insolent and insubordinate, only do the most basic tasks and do not come when called.

Lips pinched, Leonhard's mother still rushes from room to room, but without her train of helpers. She tugs clumsily at the heavy wardrobes, hissing with rage, but they refuse to budge, the cupboards seem to be screwed to the floor, drawers resist, won't open, won't close. Everything she takes in her hand, she drops and no one picks it up. There are hundreds of objects lying around, debris piles up forming insurmountable obstacles no one clears away. The bookshelves fall off the wall, engulfing the room in an avalanche of books, making it impossible to get to the window to close it. It bangs in the wind until the glass breaks and the rain pours in. Soon everything is covered in a grey blanket of mould.

The Countess is seized with fits of insane fury, hammering the walls with her fists, gasping for breath, screeching, tearing up anything she can lay her hands on. Her impotent rage at the fact that no one obeys her any longer — she cannot even use her son as a servant since he fell down and has to hobble round with a stick — finally robs her of the last shreds of reason. She spends hours muttering to herself, grinding her teeth, giving angry shouts, scurrying along the corridors like a wild animal.

But gradually a strange transformation takes place. Her features take on a witch-like air, her eyes a greenish shimmer, she seems to see spectres, suddenly listens, open-mouthed, as if someone were whispering to her, and asks, 'What? What? What must I do?'

Little by little the demon inside her unmasks itself as her mindless urge to be busy is replaced by a conscious, calculating malice. Now she leaves the things around her in peace, doesn't touch anything. Dirt and dust gather everywhere, the mirrors are clouded, the garden choked with weeds, nothing is in its right place, even the most essential utensils are impossible to find. The servants offer to clear away the worst of the mess but she forbids it with a peremptory 'No!' She is quite happy that everything is in chaos, the tiles falling off the roof, the woodwork rotting, the fabrics mildewed. She gloats inwardly as she sees those around her suffering a new kind of torment, an unease mounting to desperation, in place of the old restlessness that made their lives a misery. She no longer says a word to anyone, gives no orders, but everything she does is done with malice, to spread fear and terror among the servants. She pretends to be mad, creeps into the maids' bedrooms at night, sends jugs crashing to the floor with a shrill cackle of laughter. Locking the door is impossible, she has removed every key in the house, now there is no door she cannot fling open with one heave. She doesn't bother to comb her hair, it hangs down in tangled knots, she eats as she walks, she doesn't go to bed any more. Only half dressed, so the rustling of her clothes will not warn people she is coming, she steals through the castle in felt slippers, suddenly appearing like a ghost, now here, now there.

On moonlit nights she even haunts the chapel. No one dares to go there any longer. There is a rumour that the ghost of the dead Count walks.

She will accept no help, what she needs, she takes. She knows full well that her silent, lightning appearances arouse greater fear among her superstitious servants than a show of imperiousness. They only talk in whispers, never a loud word, they all have guilty consciences even though there is not the slightest reason.

But the main object of her machinations is her son. With insidious cunning, she uses every occasion to exploit her natural dominance as his mother and increase his feeling of dependence. She plays on his nervous fear, his feeling he is never unobserved, whipping it up into a delusion of constantly being caught in the act until he is oppressed by a permanent sense of guilt. Whenever he tries to speak to her, she just screws up her face in a mocking sneer so that the words stick in his throat and he feels like a criminal whose iniquity is branded on his forehead. His vague fear that she might be able to read his most secret thoughts, that she might know about him and Sabina, becomes an alarming certainty when her penetrating gaze rests on him. At the slightest sound he desperately tries to look innocent, and the harder he tries, the less he succeeds.

A secret longing ripening into love draws Leonhard and Sabina together. They slip each other little letters with the feeling they are committing a mortal sin. But the tenderer shoots of affection are poisoned by their sense of perpetually being followed and wither, leaving them in the grip of boundless animal lust. They station themselves at the junction of corridors where they cannot see each other but where one of them will spot the Countess if she comes and can warn the other. Thus, they talk and, afraid of losing precious minutes, speak frankly, openly putting their feelings into plain words and fanning the flames of desire even more.

But they find they are more and more restricted. As if the old woman suspects what is going on, she locks up the second floor, then the first. All that is left to them is the ground floor, where the servants are coming and going all the time. Leaving the castle grounds is forbidden and there are no hiding places in the park, even at night. If the moon is shining, they can be seen from the castle windows, if it is dark, they risk having the

Countess steal up on them.

Their passion grows impossible to curb the more they are compelled to repress it. The idea of openly disregarding the barriers between them never enters their heads. From earliest childhood they have been too deeply imbued with the conviction that they are completely at the mercy of a demonic force with power over life and death, for them even to think of looking each other in the face in his mother's presence.

The meadows are scorched by the torrid heat of summer, the ground is parched and cracked, the evening sky is aflame with sheet lightning. The grass is yellow, numbing the senses with the sultry smell of hay, the walls quiver in the heat haze. Leonhard and Sabina too are so hot with desire their whole being revolves around one thing alone. When they meet they can hardly stop themselves falling upon each other.

Then comes one feverish, sleepless night with wild, lascivious waking dreams. Every time they open their eyes they see Leonhard's mother peering in, hear her stealthy footsteps at their doors. It hardly registers with them, seems half reality, half delusion, they cannot wait for the morrow when they are finally going to meet, regardless of the consequences, in the chapel.

They stay in their rooms the whole morning, listening at the door with bated breath and quaking knees for signs that the old woman is in some more distant part of the castle.

Hour after hour passes in agonising torment, midday sounds — there! A noise like the clink of keys in the interior of the building gives them the illusion of safety. They dash out into the garden. The chapel door is ajar, they push it open and slam it to behind them so that the bolt snaps shut.

They do not see that the iron trapdoor leading down into the crypt is propped open by a wooden strut, do not see the square hole yawning in the floor, do not feel the icy air coming out of the funeral vault. Like beasts of prey, they devour each other with their looks. Sabina tries to speak, but all that comes out is a frenzied babble. Leonhard rips off her clothes and throws himself on her. Panting, they grapple each other tight.

In their intoxication they lose all sense of their surroundings. Shuffling steps feel their way up out of the crypt; they hear them clearly but it makes no more impression on their consciousness of what is happening than the rustling of leaves.

Hands appear in the opening, take a grip on the stone flags and pull up.

A figure slowly emerges from the floor. Sabina sees it first through her half-closed lids, as if through a red veil. Suddenly awareness of the situation strikes and she lets out a piercing cry. It is the gruesome old woman, the terrible creature who is everywhere and nowhere, rising from the ground!

Leonhard jumps up in horror. For a moment he is paralysed as he finds himself staring into his mother's face, twisted in a malevolent grimace, then fury breaks out in a wild, foaming torrent. He kicks away the wooden prop. The trapdoor comes down with a crash on the Countess' skull, sending her tumbling down into the crypt. They hear the dull thud as her body hits the ground.

Rooted to the spot, they stare at each other without a word, eyes wide, knees trembling. To save herself from falling, Sabina slowly crouches down and, groaning, buries her head in her hands. Leonhard drags himself over to the prie-dieu. His teeth are chattering audibly.

Minutes pass. Neither of them dares to move, they avoid each other's eyes. Then, under the whiplash of the same thought, they both dash out into the open and back into the house, as if the Furies were at their heels. The setting sun transforms the well into a pool of blood, the castle windows are ablaze with fire, the shadows of the trees turn into long, thin arms with fingers inching their way across the lawn to stifle the last chirping of the crickets. The breath of twilight dulls the radiance. Night falls, blue-black.

With much shaking of heads the servants speculate as to where the Countess might be. They ask the young master; he just shrugs his shoulders and looks away so they won't see how deathly pale his face is.

Lantern lights bob to and fro in the park. The servants scour the banks of the pond and shine their lanterns over the water; black as asphalt, it throws back the light. A sickle moon is floating on the surface. Startled marsh birds fly up from the reeds.

The old gardener unleashes his dog and combs the woods round the castle. Now and then the sound of his voice calling can be heard in the distance. Each time Leonhard starts, his hair stands on end, his heart misses a beat. Is that his mother crying out under the ground?

Midnight. The gardener still has not returned. The servants are oppressed by a vague sense of impending disaster and crowd together in the kitchen, telling each other spine-chilling stories of people who mysteriously vanished to reappear as werewolves, digging up graves and feeding off the bodies of the dead.

Days, weeks pass. No sign of the Countess. It is suggested Leonhard should have a mass said for her soul. His response is violent. He refuses; the chapel is emptied of its furnishings, only a gilded, carved prie-dieu is left in which he sits for hours, brooding. No one else is allowed to enter the building. Some say that if you look through the keyhole you can often see him lying with his ear to the floor, as if he were listening for sounds from the crypt.

At night Sabina shares his bed. They make no attempt to conceal the fact that they are living together as man and wife.

The rumour of a mysterious murder reaches the village, will not die, eats its way instead farther and farther out into the country. One day a spindly, bewigged official drives up in a yellow carriage. Leonhard remains closeted with him for a long time, then the man leaves. The months pass and no more is heard of him, yet the malevolent whispers in the castle continue. No one doubts that the Countess is dead, but she lives on as an invisible ghost, everyone can sense her malign presence.

The servants give Sabina black looks, think she is somehow to blame for whatever has happened; conversations abruptly break off when the young Count appears.

Leonhard sees what is happening, but behaves as if he hadn't noticed, puts on a frosty, peremptory manner.

In the house nothing has changed. Creepers climb up the walls, mice, rats, owls nest in the rooms, tiles are missing from the roof, exposed beams rot and crumble. Only in the library is there some semblance of order, but the books have gone mouldy with the damp and are scarcely legible any longer.

Leonhard spends whole days hunched over the old volumes, laboriously trying to decipher the smudged pages covered in his father's jerky scrawl. Sabina must be at his side all the time.

Whenever she is not there, he falls prey to an agitation almost beyond control; he doesn't even go to the chapel without her any more. But they don't talk to each other. Only at night, when they are in bed together, he is seized with a kind of delirium, and in an endless tangle of gabbled sentences, he spews out everything he can remember from the books he has devoured during the day. He knows the reason for this compulsion. It is his mind desperately struggling to stop the terrible image of his murdered mother taking shape in the darkness, to drown out with words the hideous, resounding crash of the trapdoor which keeps on echoing in his ear. Sabina lies there motionless, rigid, not interrupting, not even with a single word, but he can feel she is not taking in anything of what he is saying. He can tell from the empty look in her eyes, permanently fixed on one distant spot, what thought she cannot get out of her mind.

He squeezes her hand; it is minutes before he feels her fingers return the pressure, and it does not come from the heart. He tries to plunge them back into the riptide of passion, to return to the days before the happening and make them the starting point for a new life. Sabina responds to his embrace as if in a deep sleep and he feels a horror of her pregnant womb, heavy with the fruit of murder.

His sleep is leaden and dreamless, but it does not bring oblivion. He sinks into a boundless solitude in which even the dread images are lost to view, leaving only an agony of suffocation, a sudden blackout of the senses such as someone might feel who, eyes closed, is expecting the executioner's axe to fall with the next heartbeat.

Every morning when he wakes up Leonhard resolves to break out of the torture chamber of this memory. He recalls his father's advice to find a fixed point within himself — then his eye falls on Sabina, he sees how, desperately trying to smile, she only manages to twist her lips in a contorted grimace, and once again he sets off on a headlong dash to escape from himself.

He decides to change his surroundings and sends all the servants away, keeping just the old gardener and his wife. The only effect is to make his solitude with its lurking menace even more profound, the ghost of the past even more alive. It is not a guilty conscience for the murder that is plaguing Leonhard. Not for one second does he feel any remorse, his hatred of his mother is as intense as the day his father died. What is driving him to the edge of madness is her invisible presence as a formless spectre he cannot exorcise standing between him and Sabina. All the time he feels her horrible eyes fixed on him, he cannot rid himself of the scene in the chapel, which is like an ulcer festering inside him.

He does not believe the dead reappear on earth, but that they can live on in much more terrifying form, without visible shape, as a malign influence which neither lock nor key, curse nor prayer can keep out, that is something he learns from his own experience, something he can see every day in Sabina's behaviour. Every object in the house awakens the memory of his mother, there is nothing that has not been infected by her touch, that does not hourly summon up her image in his mind.

The folds in the curtains, a pile of crumpled washing, the grain in the panelling, the lines and spots on the tiles, everything he looks at resolves into her face. His similarity to her leaps out at him like a viper from the mirror, making his heart run cold with fear that the impossible might happen, that his face might suddenly turn into hers, a gruesome legacy that will remain with him to the end of his days.

The air is filled with her stifling, ghostly presence, the creak of the floorboards sounds as if it comes from her footsteps. Neither heat nor cold drives her away; whether it is autumn, a cold, clear winter's day or a mild, sickly spring breeze, it only touches the surface. No season, no outward change affects her, she is constantly striving to take form, to become more clearly visible, to assume permanent shape. The secret conviction that one day she will succeed, even if he cannot imagine how it can happen, is like a huge boulder pinning him down.

Help, he realises, can only come from his own heart, for the outside world is in league with her. But the seed planted in him by his father seems to have withered and died. The brief moments of relief, of peace he felt then, refuse to return, however hard he tries to revive them. The most he can do is evoke the superficial impressions, which are like artificial flowers, lacking scent and with ugly wire stalks. He tries to breathe life into them by reading the books which form the spiritual bond between himself and his father, but they remain a labyrinth of abstractions which set off no vibrations inside him.

Strange things turn up as he delves into the jumble of tomes with the ancient gardener. Parchments covered in symbols, pictures of a goat with a man's face, devil's horns at the temples and a golden beard, knights in white cloaks, their hands folded in prayer and crosses on their breast that are not formed from an upright and a horizontal bar, but from four running legs, bent at the knees — the satanic cross of the Templars, as the gardener reluctantly tells him — then a small, faded portrait, his grandmother, to go by the name embroidered underneath in coloured glass beads, with two children, a boy and a girl, sitting on her lap. Their features seem strangely familiar. For a long time, he cannot tear his eyes from them and a dark suspicion surfaces in his mind: these must be his parents, even though they are clearly brother and sister. The sudden unease in the old man's expression, the way he avoids his eye and obstinately ignores all his questions about the two children only serve to strengthen his suspicion that he is on the track of a secret that concerns him.

A bundle of yellowing letters appears to belong with the picture since they are in the same casket. Leonhard takes them, resolving to read them that very day.

It is the first night for a long time that he has spent without Sabina. She feels too weak to sleep with him, says she is in pain.

He walks up and down in the room where his father died. The letters are on the table. He keeps going to read them then puts it off, as if under some kind of compulsion.

A new, indistinct fear announces itself. It is as if someone were standing behind him with a drawn dagger, throttling him. He knows that this time it is not his mother's ghostly presence that makes him break out in a cold sweat, it is shadows from a distant past that are bound to the letters and are waiting to drag him down into their realm.

He goes over to the window, looks out: all around a breathless, deathly hush. There are two bright stars close together in the southern sky. They seem strangely alien, the sight troubles him, though he cannot quite say why, arouses a foreboding of some cataclysmic event. They are like shining fingertips pointing at him.

He turns back to the room. The flames of the two candles on the table are waiting for him, motionless, like two ominous messengers from the world beyond. It is as if their light comes from a long way away, from a place where no mortal hand can have placed them. Imperceptibly the hour draws nigh. Softly, like ash falling, the hands move round the clock.

Was that a cry downstairs in the castle? Leonhard listens. Everything is quiet.

He reads the letters. His father's life unrolls before him, the struggle of a free spirit who rebels against everything that goes by the name of law. He sees a towering Titan bearing no resemblance at all to the dotard he knew as his father, a man who will stop at nothing, a man who openly proclaims that, like his ancestors, he is a knight of the true Order of Templars, who glorify Satan as the creator of the world and for whom the very word 'grace' is an indelible stain on their honour. Intermingled with the letters are pages from his diary describing the torment of a parched soul, the impotence of a spirit with wings worn ragged by the cares of the everyday world: he is on a road that leads down, from abyss to abyss, into darkness and madness, a road on which there is no turning back.

A thread running through everything is the repeated indication that the whole family has been driven for centuries from one crime to the next. It is a grim legacy, passed on from father to son, that a woman, be it wife, mother or daughter, will always appear, as victim or perpetrator of bloody murder, to frustrate their search for spiritual peace. And yet even in the deepest despair hope ever shines anew, like an inextinguishable star, that one day a scion of our line will come who will not bow before the curse, but will end it and win the crown of 'Master'.

Pulse racing, Leonhard devours episodes blazing with his father's passion for his own sister, episodes which reveal that he is the fruit of this union, and not only he, but Sabina as well. Now it is clear why Sabina does not know who her parents are, why there is nothing to reveal her origin. The past comes alive, and he sees his father trying to protect him by having Sabina brought up as a peasant girl, a serf of the lowest rank, so that both of them, son and daughter, will remain unaware of the stigma of incest, even if the curse on their parents should return and bring them together as man and wife.

This desire informs every terror-haunted word in one letter from his father, ill in a foreign city, to their mother. He implores her to do everything possible to prevent the children discovering the dark secret, including burning his letter immediately.

Leonhard is devastated. He tears his eyes away from the letters, but they are like a magnet, drawing him back to read on. He knows they will contain things that are exact parallels to what happened in the chapel, things that will drive him to the outer edge of horror if he reads them. With sudden insight, like lightning rending the darkness, he sees the cunning strategy of a gigantic demonic power which, concealed behind the mask of blind, impassive fate, is systematically trying to crush the life out of him. One poisoned arrow after another is being aimed at his soul so that he will waste away until the last threads of confidence wither and he falls prey to the same destiny as his forefathers in a helpless, impotent collapse.

Suddenly, like a tiger, resistance asserts itself and he holds the letter in the flame of the candle until the last glowing fragments scorch his fingers. A wild, implacable fury at the satanic monster that has the weal and woe of mankind in its grasp burns him to the very marrow. His ears ring with the cry for vengeance from a thousand throats, from all the past generations that fell into the clutches of fate and came to a wretched end. His every nerve is a clenched fist, his soul a bristling arsenal of weapons.

He feels he must perform some unheard-of deed, something to shake heaven and earth to their foundations. Behind him is the numberless army of the dead, their myriad eyes fixed on him, just waiting for a sign to follow him, the living man, the only one who can lead them into battle and fall upon their common enemy.

Staggering under the impact of a wave of power that pours over him, he looks round. What should he do first? Set the house on fire, tear himself limb from limb, or charge down, knife in hand, and slay everyone he comes across?

Each 'deed' seems more petty than the other. His sense of his own puniness threatens to crush him, he fights against it in an upsurge of youthful defiance and feels a mocking grin suffuse the space around which only serves to goad him to further action.

He tries a calm approach, thinks himself into the attitude

of a general weighing every factor, goes to the chest outside his bedroom, fills his pockets with gold and jewels, takes his coat and hat and strides out proudly, without any farewells, into the misty night, his mind awash with confused, childish plans of wandering aimlessly round the world and confronting the lord of destiny.

The castle disappears behind him in the milky haze. He would like to avoid the chapel, but he has to go past it. He can feel the generations of the bloodline trying to stop him escaping their influence and forces himself to walk straight ahead, hour after hour. But the spectres of memory keep step with him. There! And there! Dark thickets yawn like the murderous trapdoor.

He is tormented by concern for Sabina. He knows this is the earthward pull of his mother's curse-laden blood in his veins trying to curb his soaring flight, trying to smother the youthful fire of his enthusiasm with the grey ashes of mundane reality. He resists with all his might, feeling his way forward from tree to tree until he sees a light in the distance, hovering above the ground at head-height. He hurries towards it, loses sight of it, sees it flashing in the mist, nearer and nearer, flitting to and fro, now here, now there. A path guides his feet, twisting and turning.

Soft, mysterious cries, barely audible, quiver in the darkness. Then the massive bulk of high, black walls with an open door rise up. Leonhard recognises his own home.

He has walked through the night in a circle.

Defeated and resigned to his fate, he goes in. As his hand touches the latch of the door to Sabina's room he feels an icy shock, an inexplicable, deadly certainty that his mother, flesh

The Short Stories of Gustav Meyrink Volume II

and bone, a corpse come back to life, is in there waiting for him.

He tries to turn away and flee back into the darkness. He cannot. An irresistible force is compelling him to open the door.

Sabina is lying on the bed, eyes closed, white as the sheets, a bloodless corpse. Beside her, naked, lies a new-born child, a girl with a crumpled face, a vacant, restless stare and a red mark on her forehead: in every feature the grisly image of the murdered Countess in the chapel.

Leonhard sees a figure rushing across the face of the earth, its clothes ripped to shreds by thorns. It is himself, driven from house and home by horror past bearing, the mailed fist of fate, no longer deluding himself with the vision of great deeds.

The hand of time builds up city after city in his mind — bright, gloomy, large, small, brazen, timid cities at random — only to crush them; it paints rivers like shining, silvery snakes, grey wastes, a merry patchwork of fields and pasture in brown, purple and green, dusty country roads, sharp-pointed poplars, hazy meadows, cattle grazing, dogs wagging their tails, roadside crucifixes, people young and old, showers of rain, the glitter of drops, the gold gleam of frog's eyes in ditches, horseshoes with rusty nails, storks on one leg, fence posts with splintering bark, yellow flowers, graveyards and cotton-wool clouds, misty peaks and blazing smithies. They come and go like night and day, sink into oblivion then reappear like children playing hide and seek when a scent, a sound, a quiet word calls them back.

A procession of countries, castles and mansions passes

Leonhard and takes him in. His name is known, he meets with friendship and with hostility. He talks to the people in the villages, to tramps, scholars, shopkeepers, soldiers, priests, and inside him the blood of his mother is in constant struggle with the blood of his father. What one day fills him with awe-struck musings, gleaming in vivid colour, like a peacock's tail made of a thousand shards of glass, the next it seems dull and grey. It all depends whether his mother or father is dominant.

Then come the dreaded long hours when the two streams mingle and he is back in his old self, giving birth to remembered horrors, and he plods on blindly, step by step, in mute silence, the space between eye and lid filled with images: the baby with an old woman's face, the ominous, lifeless candle flames, the two stars close together in the sky, the letter, the sullen castle and its life-sapping torments, Sabina's corpse with its snow-white hands. In his ear he hears the babble of his dying father, the rustle of the silk dress, the crack of a skull bursting open.

Now and then he feels a sudden spasm of fear that he is going round in a circle again. Every wood appearing in the distance threatens to turn into the familiar park, every wall into the castle, the faces of people coming towards him look more and more like the maids and servants of his youth. He takes refuge in churches, sleeps out in the open, joins wailing processions, gets drunk in taverns with rogues and whores in order to hide from the sharp eye of fate, lest it catches him again. He decides to become a monk. The abbot of the monastery is horrified when he hears his confession and learns he bears the name of a family still under the anathema pronounced on the old Knights Templar. He plunges into the maelstrom of life; it spews him back out. He goes in search of the devil. Evil is everywhere, yet its author nowhere to be found. He looks for him within his own self, and that self has disappeared. He knows it must be there, he can feel it with every second, and yet the moment he looks for it, it is gone, every day it is different, a rainbow that touches the earth but constantly recedes, dissolves, when you try to grasp it.

Wherever he looks, he sees the Cross of Satan formed from four running legs hidden behind everything, everywhere the same pointless procreation, the same pointless growing and dying, a wheel, eternally spinning in the wind, which he equates with the womb from which suffering springs, only the axis on which it turns remains, as intangible as a mathematical point.

He meets a monk from a mendicant order, travels with him, prays, fasts, castigates himself like him. The years slip by like the beads of a rosary, nothing changes, not inwardly, not outwardly, only the sun grows dimmer. As always, every last thing is taken from the poor while the rich are rewarded twice over. The more fervently he begs for 'bread', the harder the stones the world gives him. The heavens remain as hard as steel. His old boundless hatred of the secret enemy of mankind that decrees our destinies breaks out again.

He listens to the monk preaching about justice and the torments of the damned in hell — to Leonhard it sounds like the crowing of the devil. He hears him rail against the wickedness of the Order of Templars which, though burnt at the stake a thousand times, keeps on raising its head, refuses to die, and lives on, ineradicable, secretly spread over the whole world. It is the first time he has learnt anything precise about the beliefs of the Templars: that they have two gods, one up above, far from mankind, and one down below, Satan, who hourly creates the world anew and fills it with abominations that grow more loathsome every day until it suffocates in its own blood; and that there is a third god above these two, the Baphomet, an idol with a golden head and three faces.

The words burn into his soul, as if they had been spoken by tongues of fire. He cannot penetrate the depths they cover like a quivering carpet of swamp moss, but there is not the slightest doubt in his mind that this is the only path by which he can escape from himself. The Order of Knights Templar is reaching out for him, the legacy of his forefathers which no man can deny.

He leaves the monk.

Once more the dead are thronging round, calling out a name until his lips repeat it and he, gradually, syllable by syllable, as if it were a tree growing, branch by branch, up from his heart, comes to understand it as his mouth speaks it, a name, completely unknown to him and yet inextricably bound up with his whole existence, a name bearing the purple and a crown, a name he feels compelled to whisper to himself and cannot clear from his mind as it is beaten out by the rhythm of his feet hitting the ground: Ja-cob-de-Vi-tri-a-co.

Little by little the name becomes a spectral guide leading him onward, now as a legendary Grand Master of the Knights of the Templar, now as a disembodied inner voice.

Just as a stone thrown into the air changes its trajectory and plummets to the earth with increasing speed, so the name is associated for Leonhard with a change in the direction of his desires as his whole being is gradually consumed with an inexplicable, overpowering urge to find the man who bears it.

Sometimes he could swear the name was new to him, at others he has a clear memory of having seen it mentioned on a specific page of one of his father's books as the head of an order of knights. He tries to tell himself there is no point in looking for this Grand Master Jacob de Vitriaco, that he lived in another century, that his bones have long since turned to dust, but in vain. Reason no longer has the power to control his thirst for the search, the cross with the four running legs is rolling in front of him, invisible, pulling him along behind.

He searches through the registers of nobility in town archives, asks experts in heraldry, but can find no one who has heard the name. Finally, in a monastery library, he comes across the same book his father had. He reads it page by page, line by line; the name Vitriaco is not there. He begins to doubt his memory, his whole past seems uncertain, but the name Vitriaco remains the one fixed point, immovable as a massive boulder.

He resolves to erase the name from his mind and decides to head for a particular town. By the very next day it is nothing but a faint cry from afar that sounds like Vi-tri-a-co, and another road is leading him in a quite different direction. A spire on the horizon, the shadow of a tree, the hand on a milestone: however hard he tries to force himself to doubt them, they all become fingerposts telling him he is approaching the place where the mysterious Grand Master Vitriaco lives and is guiding his footsteps.

In an inn he meets a travelling quack and for a moment deludes himself with the vague hope that he might be the one he is looking for. But the quack is called Doctor Bleedwite. He is a dark-complexioned man with small, shiny, pine-marten's teeth and shifty eyes, and there is nothing in this world that he does not know, no place he has not been, no thought he cannot read, no heart whose depths he cannot plumb, no illness he cannot heal, no tongue he cannot loosen and no coin that is safe from him. The girls crowd round for him to read their fortunes from their palms or in the cards. People fall silent and quietly slink away when he whispers details from their past to them.

Leonhard drinks the whole night through with him. At times in his drunken stupor, he is overcome with dread at the idea that it is not a human being sitting opposite him. The doctor's features keep on blurring and all he can see is the white teeth, from which words emerge which are half an echo of what he has said himself, half answers to scarcely formulated questions. As if the man could read his innermost desires, he brings even trivial conversations round to the Templars. Leonhard keeps wanting to find out if he has heard of a certain Vitriaco but each time, when it is almost too late, he feels deep misgivings and bites back the name.

They travel on together, wherever chance takes them, from one fair to the next. Doctor Bleedwite eats fire, swallows swords, changes water into wine, pushes daggers through his cheeks and tongue without bleeding, heals people possessed by evil spirits, summons up ghosts, puts spells on man and beast. Leonhard has daily proof that the man is a swindler who can neither read nor write and yet performs miracles. The lame cast their crutches aside and dance, women in labour give birth the moment he lays hands on them, epileptics are cured of their fits, rats leave the houses in hordes and plunge into the river. He finds it impossible to break away from him; he is under his spell, yet thinks himself free.

Again and again his hopes that the quack will lead him to Vitriaco die, only to blaze up brighter than ever the next minute, fanned by some ambiguous remark. Everything the mountebank says and does is double-edged: he dupes people and at the same time helps them; he lies and what he says conceals profound truths; he tells the truth and the mocking face of falsehood appears behind it; he gabbles away at random and his words become prophecy; he makes predictions from the stars and they come true, even though he knows nothing about astrology; he brews potions from common weeds and they work like magic; he laughs at people's credulity and is himself as superstitious as any old crone; he scoffs at the crucifix and makes the sign of the cross when a black cat crosses his path; asked for advice, he brazenly flings the questioner's own words back in his face, yet from his lips they turn into answers that hit the nail on the head.

It is with astonishment that Leonhard sees a miraculous power revealed in this most unworthy of earthly instruments. Gradually he comes to grasp the key to the mystery. If he sees in him the swindler alone, then everything he learns from him dissolves into mere gibberish, but if he looks for the invisible power that is reflected in the quack doctor, like the sun in a muddy puddle, the mountebank immediately becomes its mouthpiece and a source of living truth.

He decides to take the risk, puts his misgivings to one side and, without looking at him, as if he were addressing the violet and purple clouds in the evening sky, asks the man if he knows the name Jacob de…

'Vitriaco…' the other swiftly completes the name, then

stands still, as if in a trance, bows deeply towards the west and, with a solemn expression and a voice quivering with excitement, tells Leonhard that the hour of awakening has finally arrived. He himself, he goes on, is a Templar of subordinate rank whose task it is to lead searchers along the mysteriously winding paths of life to the Master. In a torrent of words, he describes the glory that awaits the select, the splendour that surrounds the face of each Brother, releasing him from all remorse, from blood guilt, sin and torment, turning him into a Janus with two faces looking at two different worlds from eternity to eternity, an undying witness to the world below and the world above, a mighty human fish in the ocean of existence, freed for ever from the meshes of time, immortal both here and there.

Then he points ecstatically at the dark-blue edge of a range of hills on the horizon. There, he tells him, deep in the earth, surrounded by tall pillars is the Order's shrine, a towering temple made from druid stones, where once a year, in the dark of night, the disciples of the Cross of Baphomet meet, the Chosen Ones of the God of the Lower World who rules over mankind, crushing the weak and raising the strong to be His sons. Only one who is a true knight, a blasphemer through and through, baptised in the fire of spiritual revolt, and not one of those grovelling whiners forever cringing before the bogey of mortal sin and castrating themselves on the holy ghost, which is nothing but their own innermost self — only such a one can enjoy the blessing of reconciliation with Satan, the sole swordbearer among the gods, without which the gulf between expectation and event can never be closed.

The quack's bombast leaves a flat taste in Leonhard's mouth, his extravagant fabrications make him sick. A secret temple here in the middle of a wood in Germany! But, like the roar of a mighty organ, the fanatical tone drowns out his thoughts and he does as Doctor Bleedwite commands and takes his shoes off. They light a fire, the sparks swirling up into the darkness of the summer night, and he drinks the foul-tasting concoction his companion brews up out of herbs so that he will be purified.

'Lucifer, by the wrongs you suffer, I greet you,' is the watchword he must remember. He hears the words, but the syllables are strangely disjointed, like a group of stone columns, some a long way away from, some close to his ear. He no longer hears them as sounds, but sees them rise up as pillars forming aisles. It seems as natural as a dream where things change into others, large ones vanish into small.

The quack doctor takes him by the hand and they walk for a long, long time, or so it seems. Leonhard's naked feet are on fire; he can feel ploughed furrows beneath his soles. In the darkness hummocks swell up into vaguely recognised shapes.

Short spells of sober doubt alternate with unshakable certainty, but the firm belief that, as always so far, there is some truth behind his guide's promises gradually gains the upper hand. Then come strangely exciting moments when, stumbling over a stone, he is roused with a start to the awareness that his body has been walking in deep sleep, only to forget it immediately. Endless deserts of time stretch between these moments of startled wakefulness, diverting his suspicions from the present to epochs apparently long past.

The path begins to descend.

Broad, echoing steps hurry down.

Then Leonhard is feeling his way along cold, smooth marble walls. He is alone. As he turns round to look for his companion, he is stunned by resounding trumpet blasts, like the call to awaken the dead. He almost loses consciousness, the bones in his body vibrate, then the night is torn apart before his very eyes as the deafening fanfares transmute into dazzling light.

He is standing in a vast, vaulted space. Hovering in the middle is a golden head with three faces. He glances up at the one facing him: it seems to be his own, only younger. The mark of death is on it, yet the brightness of the metal, which half obscures its features, glows with indestructible life. It is not the mask of his youth that Leonhard is seeking, he wants to see the two other faces which look out into the darkness, wants to penetrate the secret of their expression, but they turn away from him. Every time he tries to walk round the golden head it revolves, keeping the same face towards him.

Leonhard peers round, trying to discover what it is that makes the head move. Suddenly he sees that the wall at the back is transparent, like oily glass. Behind it is a figure, arms outstretched, dressed in tattered clothes, hunchbacked, a wide-brimmed hat pulled down over his eyes, standing motionless as death on a mound of bones from which sparse blades of grass grow: the Prince of this World.

The trumpets fall silent.

The light dies away.

The golden head disappears.

All that is left is the pale luminescence of decay surrounding the figure. Leonhard feels a numbness slowly creep over his body, paralysing him limb by limb, curbing the flow of blood so that his heartbeat grows slower and slower until it finally stops.

The only part with which he can still say 'I' is a tiny spark somewhere in his breast.

With the reluctant fall of moisture from a leaf, the hours drip into a spreading pool of endless years.

Almost imperceptibly the figure takes on the outline of reality. In the grey light of dawn the hands on its outstretched arms slowly shrink to stumps of rotten wood, the skulls reluctantly give way to dusty round stones. Wearily Leonhard pulls himself to his feet. Looming menacingly over him, wrapped in rags, features made of pieces of glass, is a hunchbacked scarecrow.

His lips are burning feverishly, his tongue feels parched; beside him the embers of the fire are still glowing under the pan with what is left of the drugged potion. The quack has gone and with him what little money he had left. The fact hardly registers on Leonhard's consciousness, the experience of the night is still gnawing at the depths of his soul. The scarecrow is no longer the Prince of this World, true, but the Prince of this World himself is now no more than a paltry scarecrow: frightening to the timid alone, adamant to those who beseech his aid, dressed in tyrant's robes for those who want to be slaves and array it with the panoply of power — a puny phantasm to all those who are proud and free.

Doctor Bleedwite's secret is suddenly made plain: the mysterious force that works through him is not his own, nor is it some invisible force behind him. It is the magic power of the believers who cannot believe in themselves, cannot use it themselves, but have to transfer it to some fetish, be it man, god, plant, animal or devil so that it will shine back on them, its potency magnified as if by a burning mirror; it is the magic wand of the *true* Prince of this World, the innermost, all-present, all-consuming 'I', the source which can only give, never take, without becoming an impotent 'you', the self at whose command space must shatter and time freeze into the golden face of the eternal present; it is the imperial sceptre of the spirit, the sin against which is the only one that can never be forgiven; it is the power made manifest through the blazing nimbus of a magic, indestructible present sucking everything down to its primal depths.

In it gods and humans, past and future, shades and demons all give up that illusion they call their life. It is the power which knows no bounds, the power which is strongest in those who are greatest, the power which is always within and never without, and immediately turns everything that remains without into a scarecrow.

The quack doctor's promise of the forgiveness of sins is fulfilled in Leonhard, there is not a single word that does not come true. The Master has been found: it is Leonhard himself. Just as a large fish will tear a hole in the net and escape, so he has freed himself from the legacy of the curse — a redeemer for those ready to follow him.

Everything is sin, or nothing is sin, all selves are one common self, of that he is clearly aware. Where is the woman who is not at the same time his sister, what earthly love is not at the same time incest, what female creature, and be it the tiniest animal, can he kill without at the same time killing his mother and his own self? Is his body anything other than an inheritance from myriads of animals?

There is no one who decrees our destinies except the one, great self that mirrors itself in countless reflected selves — great and small, clear and murky, good and evil, happy and sad — and yet is untouched by joy or sorrow, remains a perpetual present in past and future, just as the sun does not become dirty or wrinkled when its reflection floats in puddles or rippling waves and does not descend into the past, nor return from the future whether the waters dry up or rain brings new ones: there is no one who decrees our destinies except the great, common self, the fountainhead from which all waters flow.

What space does that leave for sin? The malevolent, invisible enemy shooting poisoned arrows from out of the darkness has gone; demons and false gods are dead, having succumbed like bats to the brightness of light.

Leonhard sees his mother with her restless look arise from the dead, sees his father, his sister-wife Sabina. They are merely images, like his own many bodies as a child, a youth, a man. Their true life is incorruptible and without form, like his own self.

He drags himself to a pond he sees nearby to cool his burning skin. His entrails are racked with a pain he does not feel as his, but as if it were another's. All spectres, including physical pain, disappear in the face of the dawn of an eternal present which seems as natural to each mortal as their own face and is yet as wholly alien as — their own face.

Contemplating the gently curving bank and the small, rush-grown islands, he is suddenly overcome with memory.

He sees that he is back in the park of his childhood.

He has walked round in a great circle through the fog of life!

A profound content fills his heart, fear and dread have been swept away, he is reconciled with the dead and the living and with himself. From now on fate will hold no terrors for him, neither in the past nor in the future.

Now the golden head of time has only a single face: the eternally young countenance of the present, as a feeling of never-ending, blissful peace; the two others are permanently turned away, like the dark side of the moon from the earth.

He finds comfort in the thought that everything that moves must go round in a circle and that he too is part of the great force that makes and keeps the celestial bodies as spheres. The difference between the sign of Satan with the ceaselessly running four human legs and the unmoving, upright cross is clear to him.

Is his daughter still alive? She must be an old woman, hardly twenty years younger than himself.

Calmly he walks up to the castle. The gravel path is a brightly coloured carpet of fallen fruit and wild flowers, the young birch trees gnarled giants in bright cloaks. The summit of the hill is topped with a black pile of rubble threaded with the silvery stems of weeds.

Strangely moved, he wanders round the sun-scorched ruins and an old, familiar world rises again from the past in transfigured splendour. Fragments he finds here and there under charred beams fuse into a whole; like a magic wand, a twisted bronze pendulum brings the brown clock of his childhood into a new-born present, the blood sweated in old torments turns into a thousand red speckles glistening on life's phoenix plumage.

A flock of sheep, herded by silent dogs into a broad

rectangle of grey, is crossing the meadow and he asks the shepherd who lives in the castle. The man mutters something about a curse on the place and an old woman, the last person to live there before it burnt down, an evil witch with a blood-mark on her forehead like Cain, who lives down at the kiln, then hurries off on his sullen way.

Leonhard goes into the chapel, which is hidden in a jungle of trees. The door is hanging from its hinges and all that is left inside is the gilded *prie-dieu*, covered in mould; the windows are black with grime and the altar and pictures decayed. The cross on the iron trapdoor has been eaten away by verdigris, brown moss is growing up through the gaps round the edge. He wipes it with his foot and a half-eroded inscription appears in a polished strip of the metal, a date and the words:

Built by
Jacob de Vitriaco

The fine gossamer threads that bind the things of this world together gradually unravel in Leonhard's mind. The name of some foreign architect, barely scratched on the surface of his memory, so often seen during the days of his youth and just as often forgotten — that is the invisible figure who accompanied him on his circular journey in the guise of a Grand Master calling him, lying here, at his feet, changed back into an empty word at the very moment in which his mission is completed and the secret longing of his soul to return home to its point of departure has been fulfilled.

Leonhard, the Master, sees the rest of his life as a hermit in the wilderness of existence. He wears a hair shirt made of rough blankets he finds among the ruins of the burnt-out castle and builds a fireplace of bricks. The occasional figures that chance to pass close to the chapel seem as insubstantial as shadows, only taking on life when he draws their image inside the magic circle of his self and makes them immortal there. To him the forms of existence are like the changing shapes of the clouds: manifold and yet basically nothing but water vapour.

He lifts up his eyes above the tops of the snow-covered trees. Once more, as in the night of his daughter's birth, there are two stars close together in the southern sky, looking down on him.

Torches swarm through the forest.

Scythes clash.

Faces contorted with anger appear among the trees, a grumble of low voices. The old, hunchbacked woman from the kiln is once more outside the chapel, waving her skinny arms, pointing out the devil's silhouette on the snow to the superstitious peasants, staring all the time at the windowpanes with wild eyes like two green stars.

On her forehead is a red birthmark.

Leonhard does not move. He knows that the people outside have come to kill him, knows that it is the shadow with devil's horns he casts on the snow — an empty nothing he can dispel with a movement of his hand — that has aroused the wrath of the superstitious crowd. But he knows too that the body they will kill is only a shadow, just as they are shadows, mere phantasms in the sham world of ever-rolling time, and that shadows are also subject to the law of the circle.

He knows that the old woman with the blood-mark and his mother's features is his daughter and that she brings the end, closing the circle: the soul's roundabout journey through the mists of birth and rebirth back to death.

THE STORMING OF SARAJEVO

(From my war years)

Nervi, July 1908

Autumn was coming on and, as Schiller says in *Don Carlos*, the fair days in Aranjuez were over.[1] My friend Stankovits, second lieutenant in the 23rd Regiment and I, were sitting in the Window Café to see if a pretty woman should walk past.

"What are you doing today, Stankovits?" I asked, "I'm off on a spree."

"Me? I've got a private engagement," said Stankovits and at that very moment the door of the café opened and Franz Matschek, Captain in the 37th, burst in.

"Have you heard? War's broken out, war!" he cried, quite out of breath.

Well, then we both stood up, Stankovits and I, quite excited and Stankovits called for the bill in the growing confusion.

"Are you not perhaps mistaken, Captain?" I asked, stand-

---

1 As Ferdinand of Castile says in the first line of Schiller's *Don Carlos*.

ing to attention. But there was no mistake.

No writer could portray what was going on inside each of us. War, war is an awful business, now I think about it in my mature years.

I was still a very young lieutenant and I felt a twinge of sadness when I thought of my dear parents at home. Times had been so peaceful and the news of the war was a bombshell.

As is well known, at that time our supreme war lord, Alois the Third, the Benevolent, was on the throne: 'Long, long ago it was, now he's resting in his stone coffin.'

Through the close connection I had back then with a high-ranking personage — I'm sorry but discretion means I cannot name names — I obtained precise details of the origins etc, etc, of the war and thus became one of the few mortals who had a more profound understanding of that page in the history of the world.

As is well known, the declaration of war was announced on that memorable 31st of September.

It happened to be the day of the cattle show. It was to be opened on the stroke of twelve. The most splendid oxen from all the regions of the Monarchy were there with their horns wreathed in garlands and all we were waiting for was the Most High arrival of our beloved warlord.

At last, the ceremonial carriage drove up and one moment later the tall figure of Alois III could be seen from far and wide on the podium. Three steps behind him, in a uniform resplendent with gold braid, was the distinguished person I have already mentioned and from whom I later learnt everything.

Our Most High Warlord discreetly took a piece of paper

out of his back pocket and surreptitiously glanced at what was written on it:

"This bridge for my people," he could be heard muttering, "no, that's not it" and he took out another card: "Hurray!" ("No, that's not it either.")

The next was a blue one with the sentence: "Then ring out, bell, loud and clear." ("Dammit, wrong again.")[2]

A new note: "Just see to it that conditions come to a beneficial end." ("That blasted Franz[3] has mixed up my notes again.")

The Most High hand dipped into his back pocket for one last time. A red card! After a moment of dreadful tension, the voice of our ruler rang out loud and clear over the heads of the crowd, slashing the Gordian knot with one decisive heave: "I — hereby — declare — war!"

Before anyone could properly come to their senses the Monarch, with his lithe gait, had already left the podium, followed by the 'distinguished person'.

For a while the gentlemen of the General Staff, all present and correct, were completely baffled. It was only our unforgettable General of Artillery, Pot Lord of Fieldox, at that time the finest mind in our army, who, as so often in such plights, saved the situation by decisively declaring, "Something has to be done now, gentlemen."

And one moment later the national anthem was ringing out over Exhibition Square.

There was an outburst of enthusiasm such as one can hardly imagine after all those years. The cattle tore themselves

---

2 Historically accounted for, if you please.

3 'Franz' was His Majesty's valet at the time.

loose and raced round, the prime bullocks could hardly be restrained; and louder, ever louder grew the cry, "Long live Alois the Third, the Benevolent!"

Among all this, shooting up like rockets, shrill curses at the enemy rang out.

As always in such cases when the call was 'take up your arms,' the whole country was in the grip of enthusiasm within a few hours. No one wanted to be left out. Even the lowest of the low would put their gold wedding ring on the altar of the country and have it replaced by an iron curtain ring. Girls were scraping day and night. (Lint, or whatever it's called.) And as for the fine ladies, they organised a bazaar with kisses for the Red Cross. Excuse me for saying so, but everyone was having a great time. I still remember it today. Despite the seriousness of the situation we often had to smile to ourselves back then.

Yes after all it was a great time!

Well then, during that whole week of memorable date the palace of the War Ministry was lit bright as day. Outside the gates the excited crowds thronged up and down and police officers had great difficulty holding up the free movement of traffic by the sweat of their brow.

As I was later told — in strictest confidence — by the aforementioned distinguished person, for a long time the gentlemen of the General Staff could not agree against which power the war was to be fought.

"Montenegro, Montenegro," almost all of them were shouting when the Major in Charge of Research reached the letter M, and we have only the insistence of the more considered gentlemen, who kept emphasising that the required mobility of the supply column, which at that very moment was being reorganised, left much to be desired; and that especially at a point, where, after such a long time, the important thing was to add a new green sprig to the wreath of their country's fame, they had to be very careful to avoid any risk — it was thus the insistence of the more calm and collected gentlemen that we had to thank for the fact that they eventually decided on — Thessaly.

There Menelaus Karavankopoulos was on the throne and the fact that he — of low descent, as was well known — was not related to any of the other ruling houses, was the decisive factor.

Thus the die was cast.

"Alea jacta est," as our late Colonel Chiçier always used to say.

All we gentlemen were thus waiting in the barracks, tremendously excited, for the coming command from above.

We were on standby and since nine o'clock in the evening the men had been lined up in the barracks yard in full marching kit.

Finally, at seven in the morning — never in my life will I forget it — came the command: "To the railway station."

And, accompanied by the old, historical 'tattaramm, tattaramm, tattaram, tattaraa — tattaramm, tataramm, tataram' we headed off through the town.

My heart was beating fit to burst.

At once I felt I had to hum the old song: *Once I had a comrade*: 'Then a bullet came a-flying, aimed at me or was it you,' as we marched along.

One hour later we were on the train.

Our regiment (Colonel Chiçier) had as we soon realised, had orders to go to Lake Constance.

There was a good reason for that.

As was well known, before he ascended the throne Emperor Karavankopoulos, whose former name had actually been Franz Meier, had, together with his brother Xaver, commanded a band of brigands. Xaver had then gone to Switzerland and established himself as a hotelier. Therefore we naturally had to bear in mind the idea that there might be fine diplomatic threads linking Thessaly and Switzerland.

We soon realised that our regiment had the task — that was to be carried out even should it cost the last man — of preventing the two Swiss warships, the *Douceur* and the *Wilhelm Hô-Tell*, from landing: by means of all sorts of cunning ploys and pretending to be peacefully occupied catching white fish, they kept threateningly close to our part of the shore by day and by night.

Hour by Hour our Colonel received the reports from our spies in enemy country.

Oh yes, those were days of the most stressful agitation!

Then the news came that, when they heard the Imperial forces were coming, the Swiss had sent all the cows in the country, together with the blasted Alpine shepherds, to the upland pastures. Then again there came the news that the Swiss automobile-trapper, Guillaume Oechsli, had been appointed admiral and that the arrival of Field Marshal Büebli — at the moment head waiter in the Grand Hotel 'Huckster *au lac*' — could be expected any hour now since the stream of holidaymakers was already beginning to dry up.

"Those fearsome marksmen from the Vaud, ready for a hero's death, are coming, the ones who in times of peace shoot the holes in the Emmental cheese' — was the rumour that was soon doing the rounds — "the truly free Swiss who can't even stand having boots on their feet; they have to spend so much time wading round the streets of Geneva that what you might call natural shoes form on them."

Nights spent ready to die a hero's death at any given moment, days listening to the never-ending incomprehensible commands in Swiss German, the terrifying 'chacha-rachch-hoou-gsi' echoing from the mountain ridges — oh, how often did Stankovits come to me in my bivouac and embrace me in tears, saying, "I just cannae stand it ony mair, ma wee friend!"

One fine morning — I'd just lit a fag and the alarm signals rang out: tatarata, tatarata all round the camp. A surprise attack, a surprise attack was everyone's first thought. Shouted commands, NCOs running to and fro, the signals from the Artillery who were in such a hurry they wanted to go with their guns right through our foot soldiers and so on and so forth. None of us men knew whether we were coming or going. In brief it was a muddle such as is only possible — in times of war.

But soon our cold-blooded calm returned; it turned out that it was simply that the field telegraphs had given incorrect signs. With the trihedrons they'd see some special trains go through Lindau which, loaded with huge, painted sheets of metal, appeared to be transporting new, totally unknown weapons. All it was, however, was the artificial sheet-metal rainbow of Rigi, an icon of the Confederation that the Swiss treasured above all things and were now so concerned about that they were getting it into a safe place.

But enough of all that. As a conscientious chronicler I feel it is my duty to cast light on the eastern side of the theatre of war.

In unparalleled forced marches, presumably unique in the history of warfare, our first, second and third corps had advanced in an easterly direction.

As is well known, the very undesirable course the campaign took for us, despite all the glorious individual phases, was only the result of completely unanticipated chance events.

However glorious the way our Regiments by Lake Constance kept the possible enemy in check, in the east we had to deal with the most incredible adversities. Thus, for example, the ordnance survey maps never arrived from the state printing office and their absence was very perceptible in planning the campaign, etc, etc.

Misconceived interpretations of Moltke's old precept of 'March separately, attack in unity', fatefully magnified by all kinds of spelling mistakes that had slipped into the plan of campaign during the years of peace had disrupted the senses, leading to the fact that the First Corps received the ammunition and the Second the guns, and then both were sent marching separately. That wouldnae have made much of a difference if, due to an unfortunate chance, the First Army Corps had not lost its way, ending up in Transylvania, with the result that the Second Corps reached Thessaly after a march of four weeks without being able to fire a single shot and had to return home without having achieved anything. The Third Army Corps, armed according to the old principle with both guns and ammunition, had unfortunately also lost its way and inadvertently ended up much too far to the south. To such an extent did the fortunes of war conspire against us!

As far as the attitude of the enemy was concerned it was a complete mystery to us from the very beginning.

At first sight the edicts Menelaus Karavankopoulos — who, by the way is unjustly known in history as 'the Schemer' — issued to his troops, seem initially completely pointless, the products of a disturbed mind.[4] One is almost tempted to think they're just a joke, if you didn't know you had been dealing with a man who was mentally ill.

Thus, the Thessalian monarch had declared that the death penalty would be the punishment for any of his men who might dare to shoot at one of our officers, justifying this measure to his staff with the crazy sentence; "Woe to us if the enemy should be without command and the men had to rely on their own judgment alone."

Karavankopoulos' mania went so far as to employ farmers, shepherds, gypsies and the like, who even had to see to it that the telegraph wires in our (!!) part of the country were kept in order, secretly welding torn wires and the like at night, simply so that, as he is supposed to have said, "the command in Vienna should be able to have constant influence on the conduct of the war."

Can any rational person understand that?

And not only that: planks were frequently placed alongside the routes our infantry had to use — as if to make it easier for us officers, who were the ones on horseback, to cross the ditches! And if a horse really did come to harm, some

---

4 Even today our state historians are racking their brains trying to find a key to the way the Thessalian proceeded.

rascal would immediately turn up bringing a new, meek and mild, broken-in mount. At the same time the other ranks were suffering a constant hail of bullets from the enemy and the guys were falling by the hundred.

And even today it remains totally unexplained why, when our second Regiment arrived in Thessaly, the enemy population showed not the least sign of consternation or fear but simply smirked. It almost looks as if the rascals had got wind of the fact that our men had not a single cartridge at their disposal.

As has already been mentioned, by then our Third Regiment under Pot Lord of Fieldox, by means of unprecedented forced marches, mistakenly ended up too far south and in the first light of dawn the amazed General Staff saw far below them a wide valley in the middle of which stood a shimmering city with defiant defences.

The hot-blooded, heroic Pot did not waste a single second. Everything they could see — the half-moons on the cupolas — in brief its whole Turkish-Greek character — the menacing, silent fort, the soldiers in the streets in Austrian disguise (!!) and apparently (!) totally unsuspecting, all that simply had to mean that this was the heart of Thessaly and that the scheming Greek was clearly trying to outwit the Imperial forces with all kinds of deceptive traps. As silently as a cat Pot stationed his troops, opened fire at six in the morning and immediately went over to a bayonet attack, all of which led to a battle of quite unprecedented ferocity. Moreover, we must give the common soldier his due: the fellows fought like lions. The city defended itself desperately, such a struggle had not been seen since the Crusades and only the descent of darkness put an end to the murderous slaughter.

Already at four in the afternoon Pot Lord of Fieldox could see with his strategist's eye that no power on Earth could deny him the victor's laurels and sent a telegram to our Most High Warlord:

After terrible battle enemy capital taken by storm, enemy escape impossible, most humbly lay decisive victory at Your Majesty's feet.

signed: P

The despatch arrived at half-past four, at six bore the cheers of victory to all quarters and as early as seven our regiments by Lake Constance had been informed of the end of the war and ordered to retire.

We had just finished a march and, as happens to be the way in times of war, I had occupied the dining room of a posh hotel and taken off my boots to let my feet dangle a bit, causing a few dandies with their dolled-up women at the adjoining table to turn up their noses, when Stankovitz stormed in, almost totally unable to speak for tears. 'Peace settlement' was all he could say. We embraced, 'shedding tears of joy and sorrow' as the song puts it so splendidly.

What rejoicing! My comrades surrounded me and, in tears, we congratulated each other. To add to the fun, we escorted the two fops out of the place by force — we were six officers and three sergeants — and then had a wild party until the early morning.

Presumably it was the next day that a flood of dispatches came casting doubt on everything and suggesting the war would continue "since the storming of the enemy capital is based on a mistake." By that time, however, we didn't care about anything and, as things were, the matter had already gone too far: our married men were already keen to get home, so eventually we stuck by the peace agreement. The despatches were naturally then declared as 'unofficial' by the Emperor.

The point was that the contradiction in the telegrams came from the fact that it was only on the evening after the battle — and therefore too late — that the conquered capital in the Eastern theatre of war was identified as Sarajevo, the Sarajevo which for years and years had been thoroughly Austrian and had been annexed to the Monarchy under Kaiser Franz Josef.

However regretful the — one is tempted to say superfluous — loss of lives at this second storming of Sarajevo may be, the course of the campaign in general and of the battle in particular had produced such a wealth of strategic experience that it can be seen as more than compensating for the downside.

All one can say is: that's the way things are in the harsh business of war.

Sorry, but where there's light there just happens to be shade. And then the fact is that war is a necessary business — even the most sharp-minded civilians have had to accept that.

At least I for my part would never want to be without the memories of my time at war. When I think about it, stroking my martial moustache as I do so, I always have this particular feeling that you can't really put into words. It's just that you are someone and should a fireman or such see you from a distance, and that wearing His Majesty's medal, they will salute and stand to attention. And if in a public place you should step on something, no one will dare to say anything. And then, above all, the girls!

Yes, as I said, I for my part would never want to be without the memory of my war years!

CHITRAKARNA,
THE REFINED CAMEL

"Excuse me, but what is that actually: Bushido?" the Panther asked as he played the ace of spades.

"Bushido? Hmm," the Lion growled distractedly, "Bushido?"

"Well now, Bushido," said the Fox irritatedly, coming in with a trump "what is Bushido ?"

Picking up the cards and shuffling, the Raven explained, "Bushido? That's the latest hysterical nonsense, a recent sham — a particularly refined way of behaving, of Japanese origin. Sort of a Japanese equivalent of Routledge's *Manual of Etiquette*. Giving a friendly grin when something disagreeable happens to you — if for example you have to sit at a table with an Austrian officer, you grin. You grin if you have stomach ache, you grin when death comes. You even grin when you're being insulted — in that case with a particularly charming grin, in practice you're constantly grinning."

"Aestheticism, hmm, I see — Oscar Wilde — oh yes," said the Lion, sitting down fastidiously on his tail and crossing himself — "and that kind of thing."

"Well, yes, and Japanese Bushido is very much the latest thing since the Slav flood has gone down the drain. Take Chitrakarna for example…"

"Who is Chitrakarna?"

"What? You've never heard of him? Remarkable! Chitrakarna, the refined Camel who has no social intercourse with anyone — he's such a well-known figure! One day, you see, Chitrakarna read Oscar Wilde and that put him off associating with his family so much, that from then on he went his own lonely way. For a while it was said that he wanted to head off west, to Austria — where, it was said, there were such an incredible lot of…"

"Shh, quiet — can't you hear something," the Panther whispered. "Someone's rustling."

They all ducked down and lay there as still as stones.

They could hear the rustling coming closer and closer and the crackling of broken twigs and suddenly the shadow of the rock where the four of them were crouching down, started to bend and swell up to what seemed like an infinite degree.

Then it acquired a hump and finally a long neck with a hooked lump sticking out of it.

This was just the moment the Lion, the Panther and the Fox had been waiting for in order to shoot up with one leap onto the rock. The Raven fluttered up like a sheet of black paper caught in the wind.

The hump-backed shadow was that of a Camel that had climbed the hill from the other side and now, at the sight of the beasts of prey, dropped his silk handkerchief, quivering in mortal fear.

But it only looked as if he was about to flee for just one second before he remembered: Bushido! and immediately stood there, stiff and with a grin on his contorted, milk-white face.

"Chitrakarna is my name," he then said in a quivering voice, making a brief English bow, "Harry S. Chitrakarna... do excuse me if I happen to have disturbed you," all the while opening and shutting a book with a loud noise to drown out the fearful beating of his heart.

"Aha — Bushido!" the predators thought.

"Disturb? Us? Not at all. Do come and join us," said the Lion courteously (Bushido) "and stay as long as you like. By the way, none of us will do you any harm, you have my word of honour on that... my word of honour."

Now he's got Bushido himself, now all at once, of course, the Fox thought, annoyed, but put on an equally engaging grin.

Then the whole group went back behind the rock, each outdoing the other in jovial and charming expressions.

The Camel really did make an overwhelmingly refined impression.

He had a goatee with the ends pointing down, following the latest Mongolian 'it's a failure' fashion, and a monocle — without a ribbon, of course.

In amazement the four regarded the sharp creases of his shinbones and the mane round his throat carefully tied in a cravat in the style of Count Apponyi.

"Oh my God, oh my God," thought the Panther: his claws had dirty black edges from playing cards and he concealed them in embarrassment.

People of proper behaviour and tact very quickly come to understand each other and after a very short time there was the most heartfelt understanding between them so that they decided to stay together for ever.

Naturally, as is quite understandable, there was no mention of fear on the part of the refined Camel, any more, and every morning he studied *The Gentleman's Magazine* with the same quiet relaxation as he had earlier on in the days of his secluded lifestyle.

True, now and then he would wake up during the night with a cry of fear, and apologise, smiling, with a reference to the effects of his turbulent previous life.

It is always reserved to some few Chosen Ones to put their stamp on their surroundings and their times. It's as if their instincts and their senses are pouring forth, like streams of mysterious, silent persuasiveness, from heart to heart, and thoughts and ideas, which only yesterday filled one's hesitant, sinless inner being with childish fear, will perhaps even by the morrow be taken for granted.

Thus it was that after only a few months the taste of the refined Camel was to be seen everywhere.

Nowhere was plebeian haste to be seen any more.

The Lion would promenade with the regular, relaxed, discreetly supple step of the dandy — looking neither to the right or the left and the Fox would daily take a sip of turpentine, to the same end as the refined ladies of Rome used to, strictly requiring the same of his whole family.

The Panther would spend hours polishing his nails,

until they were a gleaming pink in the sun, and it sounded uncommonly distinctive when the dice snakes stressed that they hadn't been created by God but, as it now turned out, by the graphic designer Kolo Moser and the artists of the Wiener Werkstätte.

In brief, culture and style were sprouting everywhere, and modern sensibility was even making its way into the most conservative circles.

Yes, one day the news went round that even the hippopotamus had woken out of his phlegmatic state, was ceaselessly combing his hair down over his forehead in a bob, imagining he was the well-known actor Adolf von Sonnental.

Then the tropical winter arrived.

Krsh, krsh, prchsh, prchsh, krsh, prsh.

That's roughly the way it rains in the tropics at that time of the year. Only for a lot longer.

Actually, constantly and without interruption from evening to morning, from morning to evening.

And the sun up in the sky looks as wretched and dull as a piece of gingerbread.

In brief it's enough to drive you mad.

Of course, you get in a terribly bad mood at that time. Especially if you're a beast of prey.

Now, instead of making an effort to behave in as engaging a manner as possible — and that as a matter of caution — the refined Camel frequently adopted an ironically superior tone, especially when it was a question of fashion, the chic style and that kind of thing, which naturally led to ill feeling and *mauvais sang*.

Thus one evening the Raven turned up in tails with a black tie, which immediately gave the Camel the opportunity for an outburst of arrogance.

"As is well known, a black tie with tails may only — unless you have the misfortune to come from Saxony — be worn on one specific occasion," Chitrakarna had commented with a smug grin.

This was followed by a longish pause — the Panther, embarrassed, hummed a little song and no one wanted to be the first to break the silence until the Raven couldn't bear it anymore and asked in a strained voice what that occasion might be.

"Only when one is being buried," had been the mocking explanation, setting off a burst of hearty, but for the Raven all the more hurtful laughter.

And of course, all the hasty interventions such as: mourning, close friends, intimate occasion, only made the matter worse.

But that wasn't the end of it. Another time — the black-tie business was long since forgotten — when the Raven appeared with a white tie but in a dinner jacket, the Camel couldn't resist the opportunity of making the insidious remark, "Dinner jacket? With a white tie? Hm, only worn on one kind of business."

"And that might be?" was the precipitate response of the Raven.

Chitrakarna cleared his throat sarcastically, "When you're going to shave someone."

That was really too much for the Raven and he swore vengeance unto death on the refined Camel.

Only a few weeks later the changing seasons meant the prey for the four carnivores was becoming more and more scarce and they hardly knew where to get even the most essential items.

Naturally Chitrakarna was not in the least bothered by that: always in the best of moods, having eaten his fill of thistles, he would go out for walks, in his rustling waterproof mackintosh, softly whistling a cheerful tune, close to the others who were sitting by the rock, shivering and hungry, under their umbrellas.

One can easily understand the growing discontent of the others. And that went on day after day!

To have to watch someone else delighting in life while you yourself are starving!

"Devil take it!" the Raven said one evening, trying to stir things up (the refined Camel happened to be at a premiere), "why don't we chop this idiotic fop up and stick him in the frying pan! Chitrakarna!! Do we get anything out of that idiotic rush-eater? — Bushido — Bushido, of course! Now in winter of all times! What madness! And our Lion — I ask you, just look at our Lion and see what he looks like from a distance. He's like a ghost, is our Lion, and should we just let him go and starve, shouldn't we, eh? Perhaps that's also Bushido, is it?"

The Panther and the Fox agreed unreservedly with the Raven.

The Lion listened attentively to the three of them and his mouth was watering so much it dribbled down over his chin as they gave him ideas.

"Kill him? — Chitrakarna?" he then said. "Can't be done. Totally out of the question. Sorry, but I've given my word of honour," and with that he started walking up and down agitatedly.

But the Raven refused to give up. "Not even if he should offer himself up of his own accord?"

"That would be something quite different, of course," said the Lion. "But what's the point of all these stupid castles in the air?"

The Raven gave the Panther an insidious look of agreement.

Just at the moment the Camel came home, hung his opera glasses and stick on a branch and was about to say a few friendly words the Raven fluttered out and said, "Why should all of us perish: better three well-fed than four hungry. For a long time, I've…"

"Do please forgive me, but in all seriousness I must — as the older one — insist on my right to precedence," and with that the Panther — after a brief exchange with the Fox — pushed him, politely but firmly, to one side with the words, "To offer myself, gentlemen, as a solution to the general starvation, is not just Bushido but even my fondest wish; I er… I er…"

"What are you thinking of my dear, dear friend?" they all said, even the Lion (Panthers are well known for being uncommonly difficult to slaughter). "Surely you don't seriously think, we would… Hahaha!"

'What a bloody business,' the refined Camel thought as a nasty idea came to him. Awful situation — but Bushido — anyway, at least it's worked once, so then Bushido!!

With a casual gesture he dropped his monocle and stepped forward.

"Gentlemen, er, there is an old statement that says: *Dulce et decorum est pro patria mori.* So, if I may permit myself…"

He never finished.

A babble of voices rang out: "Of course, my dear Sir, you may," the Panther sneered.

"*Pro Patria mori*, whoopee — I'll give you a dinner jacket and white tie, you stupid so-and-so," the Raven squawked in between.

Then came a terrible blow, the breaking of bones and Harry S. Chitrakarna was no more.

Oh well, Bushido just isn't something for Camels.

THE DEATH OF SCHMEL
THE PORK BUTCHER

A Drowsy Story

Anyone who thinks that the esoteric doctrines of the Middle Ages died out with the witch trials or are even based on deliberate or unwitting deception is very much mistaken.

No one would have understood that better than Amadeus Veverka who on this day, with symbolical pomp and pageantry, was raised to the office of *Supérieur inconnu* of the occult Order of the Hermetic Brotherhood of Luxor and is now sitting pensive — shuddering at the teachings of *The Book of Ambertkend* — on a block of stone on the Nusle Steps in Prague, drowsily yawning into the night.

The young man mentally reviews all the strange images he saw that evening — and he hears, as if from a great distance, the monotonous voice of Ganesha, the Arch-Censor: "The first figure, over which you must say the word Hom, appears under a mixed colour of black and yellow, it is in the House of Saturn. If our mind is solely occupied with this figure, if our eyes are firmly fixed on it and we express the name of Hom within ourselves, then the eyes of understanding will open and you will acquire the secret.

And the brothers of the Order are standing around, the blue band round their foreheads and their staffs wreathed with roses. Free researchers fathoming the depths of the deity, dressed in white masks and white gowns so that none can recognise the other, none can know of the other. (If they meet in the street, however, they recognise each other by the handshake.)

Amadeus Veverka puts his hand inside his jacket to see if he still has the emblem of his new dignity: the gold coin with the enamel grape pip on it, and wallows in the proud feeling of superiority over these people asleep in the nocturnal mass of houses who know nothing better than the mysteries of the magistrates' decrees and how to eat well and drink a lot.

Counting it off on his fingers he repeats to himself everything which from now on has to be kept highly secret.

"If things go on like this," comes a whisper from that malicious inner self which enthusiastic German poets veil under the symbol of 'the Black Knight on the left-hand', "I'll end up having to keep the one-times table secret."

Naturally he sent this devil back into its dark world with a vigorous kick, as is appropriate for a young *Supérieur inconnu* and as the Brotherhood expects of him.

The last street lamp in the vicinity has been turned down and the only light over the city swathed in mist is the shimmer of the stars. Bored, they blink down on the grey city of Prague, thinking wistfully of the old days, when Count Wallenstein looked up at them from his castle on the Mala Strana, meditating. And of the way Emperor Rudolf's alchemists in their swallow's nests on the Daliborka spent the nights boiling pots and murmuring and putting out their fires in terror when Mars came close to the Moon. The times of reflection are over and Prague lies there snoring like a drunken market woman.

All around was hilly countryside. The valley of the Nusl remains in earnest and mysterious silence before the dreamy secret disciple, in the distant background the massive forests are in deepest darkness, asleep in the clearings are the rogues who have not yet found employment as detectives with the Prague Police.

Banks of white fog are dancing over the wet meadows, from far away the dreamy whistle of the railway engine wakens a frail yearning.

Amadeus Veverka thinks and thinks: now what did it say about the promised revelations of inner nature in the old manuscript that Brother Sesostris read out during the open discussion?

"If you look up into the night sky and want to achieve vision, then direct your gaze at a point you imagine in the far distance until you can feel that the axes of your eyes no longer meet. Then you will be seeing with the eyes of your soul: things serious, sad and comical they are recorded in the book of Nature; things that cast no shadow. And your vision will fuse with thought."

The young man looks out into the cloudless dark until he forgets his eyes. Geometrical shapes are there on the sky, growing and changing, darker than the night. Then they fade and pieces of equipment such as are needed in banal everyday life appear: a rake, a watering can, nails, a shovel. And now there's a chair, upholstered in green cord and with a broken arm.

Amadeus Veverka makes a great effort to replace the old arm with a new one. In vain. Every time he thinks he's done it, the image fades and returns to its old form. Eventually it disappears completely, the air looks like water and gigantic fish with shining scales and gold spots come swimming into it. As they move their purple fins, he can hear the roaring of the water.

Amadeus comes to with a start of alarm. Like someone waking abruptly. There is monotonous singing coming through the dark. He stands up: a few ordinary people. Slav singsong. 'Melancholy' people call it who talk about it without ever having heard it.

Happy the mortal who has never experienced it.

Rising up in the west is the splendid town house of Schmel the pork butcher — a real palace.

Who does not know him, that commendable man? His fame resounds across the land as far as the blue sea.

Gothic windows look proudly down into the valley.

The fish have vanished and Amadeus Veverka once more searches for the field of vision in infinity. A bright spot, perfectly round, which is expanding more and more, shines out. Pink figures step into the focal point, microscopically small and yet so sharp, it's as if they're being seen through a lens. Illuminated by blinding light, yet the bodies cast no shadow.

An immeasurable column is marching up, keeping the rhythm — and making the earth quiver. It's pigs — pigs! Pigs walking upright on their hind legs! At the front the noblest among them, the first in the transmigration of souls, who were the bravest down here on Earth — now wearing the visorless caps of the German student corps with the violet fraternity ribbon so that everyone can see in what form they will reappear on Earth.

The transverse flutes shrill, the pink figures spread out wider and wider and staggering in the middle is a dark, stooping, shadowy human figure, bound hand and foot. They are heading for the place of execution — marked out by two crossed ham bones. The prisoner is loaded down with heavy chains of smoked sausages, dragging him down into the swirling dust. The flutes fall silent, the chant rings out:

> *That is Schmel the pork butcher,*
> *that is Schmel the pork butcher*
> *that is the leathery pork butcher Schmel*
> *tara, tara,*
> *pork butcher Schmel.*
> *That is the pork butcher Schmel!*

Now they've stopped and gather in a circle, waiting for the sentence to be pronounced. The prisoner has to present what he can say in his defence. Yet every pig knows that the accused has to be told every point on the indictment. Just as in a court of honour for officers.

A gigantic boar in a bloodstained apron makes the speech for the defence.

He points out that the accused presumed he was acting in the best interest of and fervent enthusiasm for home industry when he handed over thousands and thousands of their fellows to the belly of the metropolis.

All in vain. The pigs who had been nominated judges refuse to be put off by the requirements of the statute book and mercilessly take pre-prepared sentences out of their pockets. As so often during their lives they had seen the way things are done down here on Earth.

The condemned man lifts up his hands, pleading, and collapses.

The picture freezes, disappears and comes back again. And so revenge is taken until the last pig is avenged.

Amadeus Veverka wakes from his slumber with a start — he has bumped his head on the handle of his stick that he was holding in both hands. Once more his eyes close and confused thoughts are dancing round inside his head. This time he's going to make a mental note of everything so that he'll remember it when he wakes up.

He just can't get that tune out of his head:

> *Who's that coming down from the heights?*
> *Who's that coming down from the heights?*
> *Who's that there coming down from the leathery heights,*
> *oh yes,*
> *leathery heights*
> *Who's that coming down from the heights?*

and there's nothing that can be done to stop it.

THE EVAPORATED BRAIN

Respectfully dedicated
to Voight the Cobbler[5]

Hiram Witt was an intellectual giant, a thinker more powerful and profound than Parmenides. Obviously, for not a single European spoke about *his works*.

There had been occasional reports in the newspapers that twenty years ago, using the influence of magnetic fields and by means of mechanical rotation, he had succeeded in making fully developed brains grow on glass plates — brains which everything suggested were even capable of independent thought — but this had never aroused more profound scientific interest.

Such things are not at all suitable for our times. And then

---

5 Voigt the Cobbler: this story — in which Meyrink expresses his contempt for army officers and the high social prestige they enjoy — makes use of a genuine episode in which a cobbler called Voigt dressed as an officer and used their normal commanding tone of voice to occupy the town hall of Köpenick, just outside Berlin in October 1906, and cleared out the treasury. Carl Zuckmayer also used the incident in a play in 1931; as for the recipe for zinc sulphate, it was used for the treatment of VD.

— what is the point of having brains capable of independent thought in German-speaking countries?!

When he was young and ambitious, Hiram Witt had sent off one or two of these brains, that took a great deal of hard work to create, to the great scientific institutes, requesting that they test them out, say what they thought of them.

Which, to tell the truth, is what they conscientiously did.

They had kept the things warm in glass containers, even had the famous high-school teacher Aurelian Paperflow give them basic lectures on Häckel's World Riddle — at the instigation of a highly-placed public figure, of course, but the results were so disagreeable that they saw themselves almost compelled to abstain from further attempts to educate them. Just imagine: even as soon as the lecture was introduced most of the brains had exploded with a loud bang, others for their part had twitched wildly a few times, then quietly kicked the bucket, upon which they began to stink horribly.

Yes, even a strong specimen the colour of salmon was said to have turned over like lightning, burst its glass jar and climbed up the wall.

And what the great surgeon, Professor Knacker, had said about the brains was truly disparaging: "Yes, if they were appendices you could cut out," he'd said, "but brains! In brains there are no appendices at all."

With that the new invention was dismissed.

That was years ago.

Since then, Hiram Witt has only delivered his brains to Kempinski's restaurant — fifty per cent, cheaper than the butcher in the town — using the proceeds to support himself and fund new experiments.

Then one day he was once more sitting in his study — 8 Tatarataa St., third floor — motionless as a stone statue, with in front of him a sheet of glass that was turning at such a tremendous speed in the steel axial system that it just looked like dully gleaming mist.

He had spent the whole night on the experiment, his eye fixed on its progress.

Whenever the hidden forces of nature realise that the point has come when they have to divulge their secret to the arbitrary will of a human being, then with invisible hands they close the gates of his senses to the world outside and reveal, in scarcely audible whispers, the hidden place to which they owe their origin, how they want to be summoned and how they can be exorcised: they hate idle eavesdroppers, thoughts loafing about on the threshold of consciousness, and there must be no one who shares the knowledge.

At such moments we are overcome by a furtive, alien wakefulness of the inner world and it feels as if our pulse were beating in a new, unfamiliar rhythm.

As if our breath had forgotten its own life, something other than the coarse air of the atmosphere works its way in — something liquid, unknown and incalculable — to nourish our blood.

Thus after midnight Hiram Witt — breathless, almost with no heartbeat — seemed to perceive nothing other than the shimmering sheet of glass whirling round on its axis in front of him: a thought that had issued from his body and taken on material form.

The echoing, stretched-out sounds, that nightly pass

through a slumbering town like lonely flying owls, did not reach his ear.

And the shadowy arms of the demon of sleep, emerging quietly, quietly, from the floor at the second and fifth hour, slipping from behind cupboards and doors to hit out with its gigantic black hands soft as down at human beings' still-smouldering sparks of consciousness, slid down off him, powerless.

The lumbering morning passed him by, the sun pushed his dwarfish light aside — he neither sensed it nor realised it.

From the busy street below came the shrill whistles and resounding music of the soldiers marching through the city with their golden buttons and, leading them, the symbolic ox-horn.

Twelve o'clock came and the midday bells fell with a roar over the yapping noise of the streets when, finally, Hiram Witt's hand twitched, moving into the buzzing wheels and bringing the mechanism to a standstill.

In a hollow of the sheet of glass a small human brain was now to be seen and on it, as the scholar established with a hasty glance, were the tiny beginnings of a nervous system — the start, the seed of a spinal cord!

Hiram Witt was giddy with amazement.

There! There!

At last! At last he'd found it, the last missing link in the chain: mathematical quantities, things purely of the mind, were the axes of the universe!

Nothing else!

Nothing left over, no nucleus any more around which the properties gathered, purely equilibrium — numbers giving birth — and their relationship with each other was the sole root of life. Visibility, tangibility, gravity — they simply vanish. Vanish like miscalculations!

Brain is related to the spinal cord in the same way as the force of gravity is to the centrifugal force. That was the solution to the ultimate enigma.

Oh yes, anyone who can understand that correctly and knows the simple moves can also make it visible and tangible: 'material' as the fools call it.

Hiram Witt looked round, somewhat disturbed — confused by the rage of thoughts surging through his inner being.

He had to orientate himself, establish where he actually was and his amazement was intense when he caught sight of the naked human body — over there on the wall — that he had brought up out of tiny cells over a full twenty years and now saw standing before him as a grown-up, unconscious creature. Hiram Witt smiled happily: "Another of my superfluous works! Why bother to build a body at all? If I can produce a brain and spinal cord, what need do I have for active junk like that?"

And just as the Wild Huntsman rushes restlessly onwards with his spectral hounds, his mind is hurtling along with confused thoughts into a fantastic future in which he will make heavenly bodies disappear from the realm of being, just as a factor breaks down composite numbers.

A cheer from a hundred voices down in the street rends the air. Quickly Hiram Witt opened the window and looked out.

A rogue in a soldier's hat and a baboon in officer's uniform had driven up in a cab and, surrounded by an enthusiastic crowd and a semicircle of deeply respectful policemen, was scrutinising the façade of the house.

And straightaway the two of them, with the ape in the lead, started to climb the lightning conductor up to the first floor, where they smashed the window and went in.

A few minutes later they were throwing clothes, furniture and a few suitcases out onto the street, after which they reappeared on the windowsill and continued their climb up to the second floor where the performance was repeated.

Hiram Witt immediately realised what was in store and quickly went through his pockets to collect all the money and valuables he had on him. At that very moment the baboon and the rogue were coming over the window ledge. "I am," said the rogue, I am…"

"Yes, yes, I know, Captain, you're the scoundrel who took over Köpenick town hall yesterday," the scholar broke in.

For a second the rogue was speechless then, pointing proudly at the baboon's colourful backside, said, "This gentleman is my er, legitimation."

'The backside, yes indeed, it's very much overvalued nowadays,' thought Hiram Witt, handing over just 4 marks, 50 pfennigs, a silver watch chain and three gold tooth fillings that had fallen out, saying, "That's all I can do for you."

The rogue carefully wrapped everything up in paper, stuck it in his pocket and screamed, "Bastard! Yeuch! Heels together!"

And while Hiram Witt was obediently obeying orders, the baboon and the rogue were vaulting out of the window in dignified fashion.

Down below the cheers of the policemen rang out when

the uniforms were seen again.

Sadly the scholar sat down again at the table he used for his experiments: "That means I'll have to produce six brains quickly for Kempinski's to make good the damage."

"Just a minute, I think I've still got one left from yesterday."

And from under the bed he took out a plate with a magnificent living brain and put it on the table.

He set the glass plate in motion and was just about to begin work when there was vigorous knocking on the door and at the same time the house was shaken by a dull, mighty rumbling.

Furious, Hiram Witt pushed his chair back. "Am I not going to get any peace today?"

Then the door was flung open and an Army officer followed by a few gunners marched into the room.

"Ah! So, you're the brain dude Hiram Watt? Oh! — Swine! Stand to atteeen — shun! Thumbs on your trouser seams!"

Obediently Hiram Watt stood up, at first moved his hands uncertainly over his body and then, as if following sudden inspiration, put them between his legs.

The officer wrinkled his nose. "Oh, fellow, are you crazy? Trouser seams, er trouser seams."

"I'm sorry but it so happens that my trousers are sewn from the inside; I'm not a lieutenant of the reserve, so I don't know which trouser seam you mean," the scientist replied, unsure of himself.

"What do you want of me anyway?" he said and, going on: "The Herr Captain from the town hall was here a minute

ago; or are you perhaps shoemaker Voigt from Köpenick?" —
but the officer interrupted him. "There, er, my lejitimashong."

And Hiram Witt read:

> Lejitimashong
> I hereby confirm on my Off'cer's word of honour
> that I am Captain
> Lord Fritz Rascal of Welshonbill
> signed: Lord Fritz of Welshonbill
>   Captain, Gards Reg. 1000

and saw from his first glance at the writing that the writer was
in the first stage of paralysis of the brain.

He bowed low before the Officer.

By now the rhythmical tremors that were shaking the
house had come closer and closer and eventually a cannon
inquisitively pushed its round gob in through the door.

That was actually superfluous, for the scholar was showing
not the least doubt anyway and when at one of the Captain's
hand movements a note fell out of his pocket on which the
recipe for zinc sulphate was clearly to be read, Hiram Witt
looked even more convinced.

The scholar bowed to indicate agreement.

"Where are they?" the Officer went on.

Hiram Witt point to the naked being without a brain that
was leaning against the wall.

"Is he registered for military service?"

The scholar, mystified said no.

"You're not doing your duty, you swine!" the Officer
roared and gave his gunners a sign, at which they immediately

started to clear out the apartment and took chairs, beds, clothes apparatus and, finally, the artificial human being out of the room.

"If he has to go into the army, shouldn't we insert the brain?" Hiram Witt asked in resignation and, although the Officer contemptuously said no, took the helmet off the plate.

What then appeared there was so surprising and eerie that the scholar dropped the helmet.

The brain that had been under it was no longer there… in it its place there was… a mouth!

Yes, oh yes, a mouth

A twisted mouth with an upturned angular moustache.

Hiram Witt stared at the plate, horrified, and a wild dance started inside his mind.

So the influence of a helmet changes a brain into a gob!!

Or does the cause lie elsewhere?

Has perhaps the sharp metal point on the helmet initiated a kind of galloping evaporation?

Just as a lightning conductor will encourage the radiation of electricity?

Is that perhaps the reason why the police have balls on the points of their helmets, in order to block such emanations? But no, that can't be, otherwise the consequences would have been — noticed. Noticed for certain. — Noticed for certain… The mayor of Köpenick… A baboon… Nought divided by nought equals one. Help! Help! It's madness. Help, I'm going crazy.

And Hiram Watt screamed a shrill scream, turned round and round a few times and fell down, on his face.

The Officer, the men and the gun were long since gone, the apartment empty. Hiram Witt was crouched in one corner, an imbecilic smile on his lips, restlessly counting on his buttons: Captain Welshonbill. Shoemaker Voigt, Shoemaker Voigt, Captain Welshonbill, genuine, fake, genuine, fake, zinc sulphate, genuine, softening of the brain, Captain Welshonbill, Shoemaker Voigt."

Finally the poor fellow was put in the lunatic asylum, but his madness never diminished: on quiet Sundays he could be heard singing:

"From the Maas unto the Me-he-mel
From the Adige to the Belt,
Deutschland, Deutschland über a-ha-lles
über alles in der Welt."

BEEN THERE, DONE THAT,
PRINCESS

"Good morning," said the Dandy, putting his yellow leather suitcase up onto the luggage rack of the compartment. 'Pleased to meet you,' and 'My respects,' said the two stolid and portly old gentlemen and that in strikingly friendly tones, for the dandy was very rich, as every respectable Praguer ought to know, and there was, moreover, something indeterminable about him — a kind of self-assurance that was frightening.

After no one at all had taken even a sip of the 'fresh water' that was constantly being offered with loud cries and the usual quarter of an hour had passed, which is necessary to make the layman believe that running trains was a science, the train slowly moved off.

The two dignified old gentlemen gave the sharp creases of the new passenger's trousers a resentful look.

Naturally they disapproved of such trumpery. A man of character has lumpy bulges at the knees of his trousers and wears broad-brimmed hats when narrow-brimmed ones are the fashion and vice versa. Most hat shops make their profit from people who are so firm in their beliefs.

And how affected it was to have a ring on your little finger. Why, for God's sake, do we have an index finger! That's where the signet ring belongs — and that with your grandfather's initials.

Not to mention the stupid fashion of narrow watch chains!

Mine does at least look a bit more dignified, thought the Head of Planning, looking proudly down at his decorated stomach over which the amethyst pendant was dangling.

"Could you please give me change for a guilder?" the Dandy asked the second old man, "I have to be quick and throw a tip out to the porter who carried my luggage."

Hesitantly the Senior Inspector fished out his large purse with the tightly shut brass mouth, looking as if someone was asking him for a loan of a thousand guilders.

When he opened it a lot of coins fell out, among them — Oh dear! — little Mizzi's milk tooth; fortunately, those of little Franzl and Max were in the inside pocket.

Nothing was lost, however, since the young gentleman had luck in his search and good eyes

An elderly woman was standing out in the corridor. The Head of Planning gave her a friendly greeting through the open door of the compartment.

"Who's that?" the Senior Inspector asked, curious.

"That... you don't know her? That's Frau Syrovatka, the widow of the late Head of the District Court. After he died, she's been living with her family again — you know them, of course, the Müllers in the upper New Town. I did hear that she had to give her parrot away, because it tended to reveal things when the young girls were around. Well, she won't miss it too much, she and her sisters have got everything. I ask you, they, they're well off — they're… they're…"

"Blasted petty bourgeois," the Dandy said, completing the sentence in ambiguous terms as he stuck out his chin and impatiently tugged at the side of his stand-up collar.

There was an embarrassed silence — the Head of Planning remained silent, embarrassed, the Senior Inspector spat on the floor between his boots and the young man, who couldn't hold his tongue looked out of the window, somewhat depressed, at the rise and fall of the telegraph wires flying past.

Even the train seemed to sense the general pressure and accelerated to quite breakneck speed.

That damned bumping and banging! The carriages were swinging and swaying, the windows rattling.

Soon the two older men found their way back onto the broad track of their habitual bourgeois speech. Though of course little could be understood, the rattling was dreadful.

Just here and there a few fragments of sentences reached the surface. "Of course, I wouldn't have travelled if I'd known the barometer had fallen — our Maxl — fourth form — Art History — Greek — incredible all the things the lad stuffs into his head."

"Well, take my daughter — next month she'll be twenty — nothing but skin and bone and has these stupid expressions: all the day long you hear: 'Been there, done that, Princess' totally without meaning — it comes from all these stupid modern novels — Metterlink — softening of the brain — there should be a law against them."

Clearly the young man must have suddenly been overcome by some deep concern, since he hadn't taken part in the conversation at all; rather he'd spent the time staring at the window-pull dangling down and eventually took out a notebook in which he concentrated on making calculations.

He was disturbed in this by the Head of Planning, who asked, as the swinging and swaying of the train gradually reduced, "Herr von Vacca will surely know that. Could you please tell me what that novel by Prévost is called, the one they're even putting on the stage now, in the summer theatre?"

"Demi-vierges," the Dandy replied.

"Demi-vierges, yes, that's it. I ask you, my dear Head of Planning, that kind of thing! And it's supposed to be realistic. Something like that doesn't exist at all. In the first place you don't get it in a decent home and in the second place not at all here in Prague."

The Dandy grinned.

"And you can't understand the hero of the novel at all. What is it that… that… what's he called now?"

"Julien de Suberceaux," said the young man, helping him out.

"Yes, that's right, Julien de Suberceaux — and what it is he actually does with the young woman, I can't understand it at all."

The inspector appeared asking to see their tickets, thus saving him having to answer.

"Where are you heading for, Herr von Vacca?" the Building Inspector asked affably.

"Me? I'm just going to Trautenau to see an ecstatic woman, an authenticated case."

"Well, there you've got something crazy again. Ecstasy! I ask you, ecstasy! A good helping of smoked pork, with cabbage and dumplings and a few glasses of Pils, that's the best ecstasy."

Pause.

"Pilsner, that really is a beer," said the old man meditatively.

The Dandy was about to make a vehement reply, but at the last moment swallowed it down with a mouthful of cigarette smoke — and anyway the Building Inspector quickly went over to another topic of conversation: "You really ought to have a linen cover over your fine leather suitcase, Herr von Vacca, to stop it getting spoilt."

"In that case I'd rather just get myself a linen suitcase," the young man replied irritatedly. Shortly afterwards, however, he took out a packet of photographs that he handed over to the old man saying, in conciliatory tones, "Are you perhaps interested in that kind of thing?"

The Head of Planning adjusted his spectacles and went through the pictures with a leer, handing them over to his neighbour one by one.

"That one there, the blonde, she's a sturdy woman — there's something to get your hands on there, hahaha! (The Chief Inspector happily joined in the lubricious laughter.) "But what's the problem with that one there, she hasn't got a head at all? — the skinny thing!" he went on but suddenly fell silent — why did the young fop have such a smug smile?

"That one!? That's a young lady," came the reply, "from the body alone — with no head — no one without the appropriate knowledge can recognise her."

Once more there was a long pause.

The sun had gone behind a cloud. There was grey light over the fan-shaped ploughed fields; the sharp shadows were gone.

Nature was holding its breath expectantly.

"My eldest daughter, Erna, is going to get married soon," the Building Inspector suddenly blurted out for no good reason.

General silence once more.

"Tell me, do you think nothing of telepathy — the transmission of thought — either," the Dandy said.

"You mean the new wireless telegraphy," the Senior Inspector asked.

"No, no, the spontaneous direct transmission of thoughts from one head to another: 'thought-reading' if you prefer."

"Oh don't keep going on about this Ibsen stuff — all a load of nonsense," mocked the Head of Planning. "It's known all over the town that you occupy yourself with that kind of stuff but you're not getting me into it. 'Transmission of thought' — haha! If I hadn't seen your pictures just now, I'd really have thought you were one of those fantasists!"

The young man pretended to take a photograph with his cigarette case.

"And did you photograph the one with no head yourself?" the Senior Inspector asked, "and is she something special?"

The Dandy waved his gloves and yawned — "Been there, done that, Princess."

The Head of Planning dropped his cigar, "Wha, wha... been there, Princess, wha... what?"

"Well," said the Dandy, "that's just one of her pointless sayings."

A jolt.

The leather suitcase fell down on the Building Inspector's head.

The train stops.

Trrr-autenau — Trauten-au

Trrrautenau

Fifteen minutes.

HONI SOIT
QUI MAL Y PENSE

"Hey, Freddy, what's the huge, red '29' doing over the podium down there?"

"Oh the questions you ask, Gibson! What does the '29' mean? Why are we here anyway? Because it's New Year's Eve — New Year's Eve 1929!"

The men laugh at Gibson's absent-mindedness.

Count Olaf Gulbrannsson, who was down in the hall, looked up at the balcony and when he saw the merry faces with the fashionable pointed tips of their moustaches *à la chinoise* hanging down over the elaborate balustrade, he had to join in the laughter spontaneously and shouted up to them, "Someone cracked a joke, eh? If you only knew, Messieurs, how terribly jolly you look with your Mongolian clean-shaven heads up there on the golden balcony! Like true Tartars. Just wait a bit, I'm coming up as well, I just have to escort my lady to her seat. Things are going to start straightaway: Comtesse

Jeiteles will sing a song by Knut Sparrow, the composer himself accompanying her on the harp, in brief (he puts his hands round his cheeks as if to reduce the sound) it will be ter-rib-le!"

"Really a splendid old aristocrat that Count Oscar, hugely distinguished, and the way he shoots through the teeming mass of yellow silk down there — like a pike," one of the gentlemen, a Russian called Zybin, said. "I recently had a picture of him in my hand, the way he looked twenty-five years or so ago — in tails, completely black, the way they were years ago but despite that bloody elegant."

"And it must have been a terrible fashion — the very idea of dressing in tight clothes and in black of all colours," Fred Hamilton commented. "If you had a few gentlemen standing round a lady at a ball it must have looked like ravens round a rotten carcass…"

"Your command of gallant comparisons is really beyond belief," the Count broke in; he was somewhat breathless, having just run up the stairs to join them. "But a quick glass of champagne now, Messieurs. I've just said farewell to Frau von Werie and feel like having a really, really good time."

"*À propos*, Count, who is the young girl over there?" Gibson asked. He was still looking down over the balustrade into the oval hall in which a flood of bright-red cushions, put on top of each other to make seats for the audience, shone out in delightful contrast to the golden yellow Turkish pantaloons of the ladies and the slightly darker toga jackets of the gentlemen.

"Which one do you mean, my dear Gibson?"

"The low-cut one there."

General laughter.

"That really is delightful, Gibson — the low-cut one! But they're all low-cut. However, I do know which one you mean — it's the little Chinese girl, isn't it, the one beside that Professor R. with the poorly shaven head? That is a Fräulein von Chün-lün-tsang. Ah, there's the champagne at last."

A baboon in livery had stepped forward, pointing with its shaggy hand at the shimmering curtain closing off the rear section of the balcony, in indication that the wine was now being served.

"Actually a very becoming costume for monkeys," one gentleman said — in a quiet voice so as not to hurt the feelings of the animal that had been trained by hypnosis and could understand every word.

"Especially the idea of putting numbers on the buttons; it's very sensible, it allows one to distinguish between them," Freddy added. "Moreover, it reminds one of those ridiculously warlike times twenty-five years ago…"

His remark was cut off by the resounding blast from a triton shell — the concert was beginning.

The arc lamps went out and the hall, with its delicate decoration of Japanese peach blossom and ivy was plunged in deepest darkness.

"Let's go, messieurs, it's high time, otherwise we'll be caught by the singing," The Count whispered, and they slipped out into the drinks tent on tiptoe.

There everything had been prepared: the cushions upholstered in Eastern silk set out in a circle for sitting or lying down on with little china tubs full of carnation leaves beside them, to dry their fingers on; the champagne goblets, that had just been filled with the sparkling combination of Indian soma and champagne, were held at shoulder height in loops of gold wire hanging down from the ceiling, quietly quivering rhythmically to keep the wine bubbly.

Shining down evenly from the walls of the tent was mild cold light, pouring its magical lustre over the soft silk carpets.

"I believe it's my turn," said Monsieur Choat, a Kirgisian nobleman. "Jumbo, Jumbo," he called out into the tiny megaphone on a metal rod that went up from the floor of the room and out through an aperture in the ceiling right to the top of the building — "Jumbo, Jumbo, the sphere, quick, quick."

The next moment the ape came sliding without a sound down the rod, fixed a polished globe of beryl the size of a man's head to two slings and nimbly disappeared upwards again.

The Kirgisian took out his box of mescalin and, throwing back his wide silk sleeve, asked, "Perhaps one of the gentlemen would be willing...?"

The Count skilfully administered an injection in his arm with a Pravaz syringe. "Right then, that ought to do for one or two visions."

Monsieur Choat pushed the beryl globe up a little higher, so that he could comfortably fix his eyes on it, and leant back. "Right then — on what should I concentrate my thoughts, gentlemen?"

"On the new prophet in Shambhala — scenes from the arena in Rome — Buddha in the order of the Foundation in the monastery garden in Kaushambi," they all shouted at the same time; each one wanted something different.

"How would it be if for once you were to try to find out where Paradise may actually have been?" Count

Oscar suggested.

Gibson used the opportune moment to slip out of the tent unnoticed — he was absolutely fed up with this new sport of vision gazing; and what came out of it? Vibrantly colourful hallucinations, that each person described in as lively a way as they could, but what it actually was — subconscious thoughts reflected in the beryl or forgotten imaginings from an earlier existence — no one was able to say.

He went to the balustrade and looked down.

Chords on the harp mingled with disconnected sung notes, occasionally accompanied by the abrupt flash of a spark of light — red, blue, green — fluttered through the darkness. Modern music!

He listened intently to these exciting wake-up calls that in a strangely jerky way were breaking on his heart, as if with the next beat of his pulse they were about to break through the walls of his soul, scraped thin by life, to some new ecstasy beyond belief.

The hall below lay in darkness, only the diamond brooches in the hair and on the necks of the women and girls glittered as they threw out the light of tiny radium pearls, that smouldered with a greenish light, like glow worms on bosoms shimmering with powder of opal.

The gentlemen were standing behind their ladies, un-moving and here and there one could see the glitter of their gilded fingernails when, fanning the air to cool their brows, they came very close to phosphorescent hair ornaments.

Gibson was making an effort to find the place where Fräulein von Chün-lün-tsang must be sitting. That very day he wanted to ask the Count to introduce him to her — but at that moment someone gasped his arm and politely drew him back into the tent.

"Oh, sorry my dear Gibson, if we're disturbing you, but you are very knowledgeable about sacred books and Monsieur Choat has such remarkable visions and thinks they might relate to Paradise — the Garden of Eden."

"Yes, just imagine, it was an infinitely luxuriant landscape from before the Flood that appeared to me," the Kirgisian said, "and that with a northern light, unbelievably magnificent — white with pink edges like lace hanging down from the sky, and the sun, a blazing red, went along the horizon without setting; it was as if the firmament were going round and round in a circle, and…"

"Those are all the signs of the zodiac in the Arctic circle, aren't they — just imagine, the cradle of mankind in the North Pole," Count Oskar broke in: "Moreover there was in fact a tropical climate up there in the days of old."

Gibson nodded his head. "Do you know that all that's remarkable — now just a minute, what does it say in the *Zend Avesta*? Oh yes: 'There they saw the Sun, the stars, the Moon just coming and going once in the year' and: 'a year seemed to be one single day.' Also in the *Rig Veda* it says that back then the dawn appeared in the sky for days before the sun rose again" (the men nudged each other: what an incredible memory the fellow has), "and then even Anaximenes says…")

"Oh please do stop giving us your learning," Freddy cried, throwing back the curtain. "Ah, the music's finished."

Dazzling brightness streamed in.

A babbling, bubbling, pattering noise filled the hall, going on and on.

"What applause, gentlemen! Just look at the way the opal powder is rising — there's a real cloud of it coming up over the balustrade"

"A truly remarkable fashion, this way of applauding," someone said. "That it's decent, would not be…"

"Yes, and how it must hurt — I wouldn't want to be a lady, definitely not — by the way, Count, do you know who was the one who invented this fashion?"

"I can tell you precisely who it was," the latter said with a laugh. "It was years ago that Princess Juppihoy, a very corpulent lady, bet that the crowd wouldn't copy her — and she had not only the *courage* for it but also the *décolletage*. You can just imagine the horror it caused back then."

Once more the *babbling, bubbling, pattering* noise came up out of the hall.

The small group stood there in reflective silence.

"Why aren't the gentlemen allowed to join in the applause?" Gibson suddenly asked in dreamy tones.

After a moment of bafflement they all broke out into a roar a roar of tumultuous resounding laughter.

Gibson blushed. "But I didn't mean it in that way at all — *honi soit qui mal y pense*."

The amusement redoubled; Fred Hamilton was twisting and turning on his cushion, "Ha, ha,ha , for God's sake stop it, it'll be the death of me. I have the feeling you were thinking of your little Chinese woman.

A resounding stroke on the gong echoed round the building.

The Count raised his glass: Messieurs, if you don't want to raise your glasses with me, then at least listen — he was laughing so much he could hardly go on — "Messieurs, 12 o'clock has just struck — please raise your glasses: all the best for the New Year, for 1929."

THE WHOLE OF EXISTENCE IS
BLAZING A VALE OF WOE

At six o'clock it's long been dark in the prisoners' cells of the District Court for candles are not allowed there and, anyway, it was a winter evening — misty and starless.

The warder with his heavy bunch of keys went from door to door, shone his light for one last time through the little barred openings, as is his duty, and assured himself that the iron bars were in place. Finally, the sound of his steps died away and the repose of misery lay over all the unfortunate ones who, robbed of their freedom — always four together — slept on their wooden benches in the miserable cells.

Old Jürgen was lying on his back and looked up at the little prison window shimmering out of the darkness. He counted the slow strokes of the discordant bell in the tower and wondered what he would say before the jury in the morning and whether he would be acquitted.

The sense of outrage and wild hatred that he, who was

111

completely innocent, had been kept locked up for so long, had pursued him into his dreams in the first few weeks and he had often been so despairing he had felt like crying out loud.

But the thick walls and the confined space — hardly five steps long — force the pain into you and don't let it out; had followed him into his dreams in those first few weeks, and he had often felt like screaming out loud with despair; then you just lean your forehead against the wall or get up onto the wooden bench in order to see a strip of blue sky through the dungeon grating.

Now these feelings had died down and other concerns, such as a free person doesn't know, oppressed him. Whether he would be released or condemned the next day didn't even make him that worked up any more. He was an outcast, what was left to him other than begging and stealing!

And if he was condemned, he would hang himself — at the first opportunity, fulfilling the dream he'd had during the first night behind these blasted walls.

His three cell-mates had been lying there quietly for ages now; they had nothing to look forward to and sleep was the only thing that shortened the long jail sentences. He just couldn't get to sleep, however, his dismal future and dismal pictures of the past went through his mind: when he was first put in prison he had still possessed a few coppers, he'd been able to improve his lot, buying himself a sausage and some milk now and then, sometimes even a stub of candle, as long as he could stay with those being held on remand. Later on they'd put him in with the condemned prisoners because that suited them better and in those cells night fell pretty quickly — the night of the soul as well.

You sit there all day long, brooding, elbows on your knees, the only interruption coming when the warder opens the door and a prisoner silently brings in the jug of water or the tin pots with the cooked peas.

There he'd spent hours brooding over who could have committed the murder and it had become ever more clear to him that it could only have been his brother who'd done it. The lad had disappeared so quickly — and that wouldn't be without reason.

Then he thought about the trial the next day and the lawyer who was to defend him.

He didn't think much of him. The man had always been so distracted, only half listening to him and making such an obsequious bow when the examining magistrate had joined them. But clearly that was just part of the whole business.

From afar Jürgen could hear the rattle of the cab that always drove past the court building at the same time. Who could be in it? — A doctor — an official perhaps. How sharp was the clatter of the hooves on the cobbles!

The jury had found Jürgen not guilty — because of a lack of evidence — and now he was going back down to the cell for the last time. The three prisoners watched dully as, with trembling hands, he attached an old collar to his shirt and put on his shabby thin summer suit, that the warder had brought. The prison clothes, in which he'd suffered for eight months, he threw with a curse under the bench. Then he had to go to the office by the gateway, the jailer wrote something down in a book and released him.

Everything out in the street seemed so strange to him: the

people hurrying past who could go wherever they wanted and took that as merely a matter of course, and the icy wind, that almost blew him over. He felt so weak he had to hold on to a tree by the road and his eye was caught by the inscription over the archway:

"Nemesis bonorum custos."[6] Now what could that mean?

The cold made him tired; trembling he dragged himself along to a bench among the bushes in the park and fell asleep weary, almost fainting.

When he woke he was in the hospital — they'd amputated his left foot because it had frostbite.

Two hundred guilders had come to him from Russia — presumably from his brother who must have had pangs of conscience — and Jürgen rented a cheap shack under a bridge in order to sell songbirds. His was a miserable and lonely life and he slept in a shed made of planks inside his wretched shop.

When the children of the farmers came into the town in the morning he bought the little birds they'd caught in snares and traps for a few coppers then put them in the dirty cages with the others.

Hanging down from a hook in the middle of the vault was an old plank on which a mangy monkey squatted — Jürgen had got him from his neighbour who ran a junk shop, in exchange for a nuthatch.

6 Fate looks after the good — the Latin quotation was the title of the first book published by the Czech writer Stanislav Kostka Neumann in 1895. Angelo Maria Ripellino says in *Magic Prague* (p.33) that Kafka's father 'hobnobbed with anarchist poets and writers, men like… Stanislav Kostka Neuman…'

Day after day the schoolboys would spend hours standing at the window staring at the monkey that shifted restlessly to and fro, grumpily baring its teeth whenever a customer opened the door.

Usually no one came after one o'clock and then the old man would sit on his stool, staring gloomily at his wooden leg and wondering what the prisoners might be doing at the moment, and the examining magistrate and whether the lawyer was still crawling to him.

When the police officer who lived in the neighbourhood walked past, he would most have liked to get up and give him a few with the iron rod over his blasted colourful uniform.

Oh God, if only the people would rise up and slay the scoundrels, capture the poor devils and punish them for deeds they themselves do secretly and with pleasure.

The cages, stacked up on top of each other against the walls, went almost up to the ceiling and the little birds would flutter their wings if anyone came too close. Many of them would perch there, sad and still and next morning would be lying dead on their backs, hollow eyed.

Jürgen would then dump them in the slops bucket — they didn't cost much — and since they were songbirds they didn't have any beautiful plumage that could have been used in some way.

Once a student had come asking for a magpie and once he had left Jürgen, who felt a bit odd that day, he noticed that this customer had left a book lying there.

Although it was in German, but translated from the Indian language as it said on the title page, he could understand so little of it that he had to shake his head. There was just one verse he kept whispering over and over again because it made him feel so melancholy:

> *The whole of being is a vale of woe.*
> *Whoever sees this with wisdom's eye*
> *Will soon be sated with this life of woe*
> *That is the road to purification.*

When his eye fell on all the little prisoners sitting, wretched, in their cramped cages it pulled at his heartstrings and he shared in their feelings, as if he were a bird as well, mourning the loss of its open fields.

His soul was filled with profound sorrow, bringing the tears to his eyes. He gave the birds some fresh water and shook out fresh food for them, which he usually only did early in the morning.

As he did so he couldn't stop thinking about the rustling green woods in the brightness of the golden sun, which he'd long forgotten like the old fairy-tales of his early days as a boy.

His memories were disturbed by a lady, accompanied by a servant who was carrying a few nightingales.

"I bought these from you," she said, "but as they sing so rarely, you'll have to blind them for me."

"What? Blind them?" the old man stammered.

"Yes, blind them. Put out the eyes with a needle or by burning them or however one does it. You as a dealer in birds must know that better than I. If a few should die in the process, that's no problem, you can simply replace them with others. And send them back to me as soon as possible. You do have my address, don't you? Adieu."

Jürgen thought for long time and didn't go to bed. He spent the whole night on his stool and didn't even get up when his neighbour, the junk dealer, puzzled that his shop had stayed open so long, tapped on the window.

He could hear a fluttering in the cages in the darkness and felt as if little white wings were knocking at his heart asking to be let in.

When morning broke, he opened the door and went out, hatless, as far as the empty market square and looked up at the awakening sky for a long time.

Then he went quietly back into his shop, slowly opened the cages — one after another — and if a bird didn't fly out straightaway he took it out in his hand.

Then they fluttered round the old vault, all the little nightingales, siskins and robins until Jürgen, with a smile, opened the door and let them out into the open, into the airy, divine freedom.

He watched them go until they were out of sight, and thought of the green, rustling woods in the golden sunshine. He untied the monkey and took down the plank from the ceiling, revealing the big iron hook.

He made the rope into a noose, tied it to the hook and put it round his neck. Once more he ran the sentence from the student's book through his mind then pushed away the stool he was standing on with his wooden leg.

THE STORY OF
ALOIS THE LION

Was thus: his mother had given birth to him and had died immediately.

He had tried in vain to wake her up with his round paws that were as soft as powder puffs, for he was dying of thirst in the scorching midday heat.

"The sun is going to drink up his life the way it laps up the dewdrops in the morning," the wild peacocks up on the ruined temple murmured pompously fanning out their tails in a rustle of shimmering steely blue.

And that was bound to have happened had the Emir's flocks of sheep not come along.

Then, however fate turned aside.

"Shepherds we don't have — touch wood — that are allowed to interfere," the sheep said, "so why shouldn't we take this young lion along with us?"

"Well I'm sure Widow Bovis will be happy to do it, after

all bringing up children is her passion. Since her eldest ram got married in Afghanistan (to the daughter of the Prince's senior ram) she feels a bit lonely anyway."

And Mrs Bovis said not a word, took in the lion cub, suckled and looked after him — along with Agnes, her own child.

Only Mister Baa-baa Ceterum from Syria — black locks and bandy back legs — was against it. Putting his head on one side, he said in melodic tones, "Fine things are goin' tae come oot ae that," but since he was an incorrigible know-all, no one bothered about him.

— The little lion grew at an astonishing speed, and was given the name of 'Alois'.

Mrs Bovis stood there, wiping the tears from her eyes now and the Communal Wether wrote an "Alois +++" down in the Book — the three crosses instead of a surname. However, since anyone could see that it was probably an illegitimate birth, he wrote it on a separate piece of paper.

Alois' childhood flowed along like a little stream.

He was a good boy and never — apart from certain secret activities perhaps —gave cause for complaint. It was touching to see him grazing ravenously with the others and laboriously chewing on the yarrow, that kept getting stuck round his long teeth.

Every afternoon he went to play with little Agnes and her friends in the bamboo copse and there was no end to their joking and jollity.

"Alois," you kept hearing then, "Alois, show me your claws, please, please," and when he really stretched them

120

out, the little girls all blushed and, giggling, put their heads together and said, "Yeuch, how gross;" — but they still wanted to see them again and again.

Early on Alois very quickly developed a deep attachment to little, black-haired Scholastica, Baa-baa Ceterum's dear daughter.

He could sit beside her for hours and she would weave him a crown of forget-me-nots.

If they were entirely alone, he would recite the beautiful poem to her:

> *Little Lamb who made thee*
> *Dost thou know who made thee*
> *Gave thee life and bid thee feed*
> *By the stream and o'er the mead*

And when he did, she shed tears of profound emotion. Then they would gambol again through the lush green until they fell over.

If he came home in the evening, hot from their childish play, Mrs Bovis would always say, thoughtfully looking at his mane, "Young folk are always the same," and "You look completely dishevelled again my, lad."

(She was so good.)

Alois grew into an adolescent and learning was his joy. He was a model pupil at school, always standing out through his diligence and good behaviour and he always had top marks in Singing and Rhythmical Dancing.

"And yes, Mama," he was always saying when he came home with praise from his teacher, "and yes, I can become head of a theatre when I grow up, can't I?'

Every time he said that Mrs Bovis had to turn away and shed a tear. "He doesn't know yet, the dear lad, that only a real sheep can do that." Then she would stroke him, give him a wink full of promise and watch him, moved, when, tall as he was, with his slightly thin neck and the soft knock knees of adolescence, he went back out to do his school work.

Autumn came across the land, and one day they were told, 'Children be cautious, don't go so far out walking, especially not at twilight — we're coming to a dangerous region now, the Persian lion, you see, goes around murdering and throttling animals here.'

And the Punjab became ever wilder and the look on its face ever darker.

The stone fingers of the mountains of Kabul dig into the valleys, jungles of bamboo bristle like hair standing on end and the fever demons with lidless eyes hang lethargically over the swamps breathing out swarms of poisonous midges into the air.

The flock went through a narrow pass, fearful and silent, deadly danger behind every rock.

Then a dreadful hollow sound made the air quiver and the flock stormed off in wild, blind fear.

From behind a rock a broad shadow shot out at Mr Baa-baa Ceterum, who wasn't going away quickly enough.

A huge old lion!

Mr Ba-baa would have been hopelessly lost if something remarkable had not happened at that point. Crowned with daisies, a bouquet of dahlias behind his ear, Alois came galloping past with a thunderous, "Baa-baa."

The old lion held back from his jump, as if struck by lightning, and stared, mightily amazed, at the fleeing sheep. For a long time he couldn't make a sound and when he finally let out a furious roar, Alois' "Baa-baa" already came from a far distance.

For a whole hour the old lion stayed there pondering; everything he'd ever heard about hallucinations went through his mind.

In vain!

Nightfall is quick and cold in the Punjab; shivering, the old lion buttoned himself up and went to his cave.

But he couldn't get to sleep and when the gigantic greenish cat's eye of the moon stared through the clouds, he got up and set off after the flock that had fled.

It was towards morning when he found Alois, the flowers still in his hair — sweetly slumbering behind a bush.

He put a paw on his breast and Alois woke up with a horrified "Baa!"

"Sir, don't keep on saying 'baa'. Are you crazy? You're a lion, for God's sake," the old lion roared at him. "I'm afraid you're wrong there," Alois replied shyly, "I'm a sheep."

The old lion was shaking with rage. "Are you perhaps trying to pull my leg? Be a good fellow and go and tease Mrs Blaschke for me…"

Placing his paw on his heart, Alois looked him innocently in the eye and said, deeply moved, "On my word of honour — I'm a sheep."

At that the old lion was horrified at how far his tribe had sunk and got Alois to tell him the story of his life.

"All of that," he then said, "is a complete mystery to me,

but what is certain is that you're a lion and not a sheep. And if you still refuse to believe it — for God's sake! — just compare the reflections of the two of us in the water here. And now you're going to learn to roar properly — like this: Waaah, waaaah."

And he roared so loud that the surface of the water became quite disturbed and looked like emery paper.

"Now you try, it's quite easy."

"Uah," said Alois timidly, choking, and had to clear his throat.

The lion, irritated, looked up to the heavens. "Well, as far as I'm concerned you can practise when you're alone. I have to go off home now."

He looked at the clock. "Oh my God! Already half past four again. Cheerio then," and with a brief wave of his paw he disappeared.

Alois was dazed — so that was it after all!

It was only a very short time since he'd left the high school — and he had it in black and white that he was a sheep — and now this!

Now when he was to devote himself to the dramatic arts.

And… and… Scholastica!

He had to cry… Scholastica!!

It was so beautiful the way they'd arranged everything, how he would go to Papa and Mama and so on.

And Mama Bovis had said to him, quite recently: "Old Baa-baa, you just keep buttering him up, he's got tons of money, he'd be just the father-in-law for you with your enormous appetite." And the events of the last few days went through Alois' mind: the way he'd praised Mr Baa-baa's radiant health and his wealth: "As I've heard, Mr Baa-baa Sir, you've kept up a flourishing export business with drumsticks and that, so I've been told, is the foundation of your wealth?"

"I have done some business in that way," Mr Baa-baa had replied somewhat hesitantly, but giving him a truly suspicious sideways glance.

'Could I perhaps have said something stupid there?' had been Alois' immediate thought, but it is generally well-known…

A noise startled him out of his dream. So, everything, yes everything was over now!

Alois laid his head on his paws and cried long and bitter tears.

One day and one night passed and he had come to a decision.

Worn out from lack of sleep and with deep shadows under his eyes he went to the flock, stood there right in the middle of them, stood up majestically and cried, "Waah wah!"

Laughter broke out all round.

"Sorry, what I meant was," Alois stammered in embarrassment, "I just meant to say… you see I'm a lion."

There was a moment of surprise, silence all round, then the noise broke out again, derisory remarks, warning cries, loud laughter.

The tumult only died down when Reverend Simulans came over and in severe tones ordered Alois to follow him.

It must have been a long, serious conversation the two of them had, for when they came out of the bamboo thicket together the Vicar's eyes were bright with pious zeal. "Just thou take heed, my son," were his last words, "many are the wiles of the evil enemy. Day and night doth he tempt us to kick against the pricks, while we do walk in the flesh down here on earth. Behold that should be all our endeavour down here on Earth, to cast out our inner Lion and spend our days in humility that a new bond may be forged and our pleas may be heard — both here in time and there in eternity.

And thou must forget what thou heard at the pool yestermorn; it was not reality but fiendish sorcery of the Evil Enemy. Anathema!

And one more thing, my son. To marry is good and will drive away the dark urges of the flesh, that are pleasing to the Devil, so woo thou the maid Scholastica Ceterum and may ye be as numerous as the sand by the sea."

He raised his eyes to Heaven. "That will help thou to bear the burden of the flesh and —" (at this his speech became song:)

> *"Learn ye to suf-fer*
> *with no be-wailing."*

And with that he strode hence.

Alois' eyes were filled with tears.

For three whole days he said not a word, he was just restlessly clearing his inner being of all impurities and when one night a lioness appeared to him in his dreams, claiming to be his mother and spitting contemptuously three times before him, he went, head held high, to see the Vicar — rejoicing that the traps of the Devil had been now put behind him and that from now on he could let thinking be and submit all the more blindly to the guidance of His Reverence.

The Vicar for his part recommended him strongly as worthy of the hand of the maid Scholastica to her parents.

At first Mr Ceterum would have nothing of it, was furious and said, "He's nothing, he's got nothing," but eventually his wife found the key to his heart: "Darling," she said, "What do you actually want, what have you got against Alois. Look — after all he is *blond*."

And the wedding was held the next day.

Baa

THAT — HOWEVER

My dear friend Warndorfer,

Unfortunately you weren't in when I called and I couldn't find you anywhere else, so I have to ask you by letter to come to see me this evening — with Zavrel and Dr Roloff.

Just imagine, Professor Beidjgriez from Sweden (surely, you've read about him?) spent an hour with me yesterday in the *Lotos Society* debating about spiritualist phenomena, and I've invited him for today — and he's coming.

He's keen to get to know you all and I imagine that if we put him under cross-fire we can win him over to our side, thus performing a great service for humanity.

So, you're definitely coming, aren't you? — (Doctor Roloff shouldn't forget to bring the photographs with him.)

In haste
your honest friend
Gustav

After supper the five men had retired to the smoking room. Professor Bejdigriez was playing with the head of a hedgehog fish on the table that was used as a match holder.

"What you have been telling me there, Herr Doctor Roloff, sounds really strange to the non-specialist, but the circumstances you quote in support of your claim that one can, as you might say, photograph the future, are definitely not conclusive.

On the contrary, they allow a much more obvious explanation. To summarise: your friend, Herr Zavrel claims to be a so-called medium, so that means that the mere fact that he is in the vicinity could be enough for certain persons to produce unusual phenomena which, while being invisible to the naked eye, can be recorded photographically.

So now, gentlemen, you have photographed an apparently quite healthy person and while developing the plate…"

"Yes, while the plate was being developed a lot of scars appeared which, just two months later, two months I say, developed on the skin of the person concerned as the result of smallpox," said Doctor Roloff.

"Right, right Herr Doctor, but just let me finish. Assuming, this was not just a coincidence… sorry, gentlemen, I just meant… so… not just a coincidence, how can you prove from these facts that here — you were photographing the future?! What I'm saying — moreover your experiment is by no means new — is that the optical lens was just much sharper, it simply saw more than the human eye, it saw the pustules in the developmental stage, the same pustules which only, as we say, 'broke out'— that is became acute — one or two months later."

Jubilant, the Professor looked round, revelling in the baffled looks on his opponents' faces before starting to suck strongly on his cigar, that had almost gone out, watching out of the corner of his eye for its brighter glow.

"Yes..." now it was Zavrel who was speaking, "but how do you explain the following, Herr Professor? One day we photographed a young man — we didn't know much about him, he was just someone we met over a coffee in the café and we would never have thought of experimenting with him if Gustav hadn't — actually with nothing at all to base it on — seen something quite special about him, sensed he might produce something of use for our scientific research. So, we take the photograph and on the picture there, right in the middle of his forehead, is a black mark."

There was a brief moment of silence.

"Well then?" the philosopher asked.

"Then a fortnight later the young man killed himself — by shooting himself in the forehead.

Look, here, in that very place — you have both photographs there: that one as a corpse and this one a fortnight before. Compare them for yourself."

For a few minutes Professor Bejdigriez was sunk in thought, his eyes as blank as blue wrapping paper.

"We've got him this time," Wärndorfer whispered, rubbing his hands.

Then the Professor woke from his pondering and asked, "Did the young man ever see the photograph with the mark n his forehead? —Yes? — Well, the whole business is quite clear now: the man was already thinking about suicide. You showed him the picture and he, well aware that it was an experiment to do with mediums, took — subconsciously — a suggestion from it. That's not to say that he killed himself because of it, no, but he shot himself through the forehead, not being aware, of course, that the idea of doing it that way had been born in him when he saw the picture. Had he not seen the print then he would perhaps have chosen a different way of killing himself — drowning, hanging, poison, that kind of thing.

"And the mark, the mark on the photo, Herr Professor?"

"The mark? That'll just be shadow, a speck of dust on the lens, perhaps an insect flying past, or something wrong with the plate. In short you won't get anywhere with proofs like that with a research scientist like me — neither of these cases is conclusive."

The friends sat there, disconsolate, letting Professor Bejdigriez' eloquence flow over them. He, for his part, seemed to be truly revelling in his victory.

"If only we could find something to use against the fellow's arguments," their host whispered to Doctor Roloff, "Just see how revolting he is with his pretentious waffle; with that short moustache and the clipped beard on his chin he looks as if he has a black padlock hanging down under his nose. Revolting fellow — perhaps he's not Swedish at all. —"

"Bejdigriez! — Professor Arjuna Bejdigriez!"

"Don't get yourself too worked up," said Roloff — calming his friend down, while Wärndorfer was trying, by the sweat of his brow, to put across to the Professor concepts of art that were at least half decent, even though he refused to believe in spiritism — "just don't get worked up, perhaps… Oh my God, are we all crazy? — We haven't told him anything at all about the main thing! — You guys: the image without a head!"

"The image with no head— hurray!" they all cried. "That was our first and best experiment — now just listen, Herr Professor."

"Me, me, let me tell it," Gustav cried in jubilation. "Do you know a certain Hellmut Schimozzle here in the town? Herr Professor? No?

"That doesn't matter anyway. He's a newspaper editor now but back then he was a clerk in a chicory business. It was sixteen years ago and we were just starting out on our mediumistic-photographic experiments. Devil only knows how we came across that ass but, to be brief, we'd had our eye on him and decided, however much he protested, to photograph him in magnesium light during a séance.

"Nothing at all had happened during the séance itself, not the least phenomenon — so the result on the plate was all the more strange. I'll get the picture out so that you can see for yourself. The negative 'came' quickly in the developer but — we were speechless — the head was missing– no trace of it — it simply wasn't there."

"Probably…" the Professor broke in.

"Just listen to what came next. We discussed it this way and that and, since we came to no conclusion, we carefully wrapped the negative up and the next day took it to Fuchs — professional photographer just across the road… on Obstgasse.

"And he uses the sharpest chemical developers to get as much as possible out of his negatives.

"And yes, clearer and clearer there appear above the shirt collar in the picture, where the head should have been, thirteen splotches of light, all the same size: and, you see, they were arranged in this way: one two; one two; four and one! Precisely the usual arrangement of heavenly bodies in the constellation of the Great Ass.

"Are you convinced now, Professor? The symbolic meaning simply cannot be misunderstood."

Professor Bejdigriez looked somewhat embarrassed. "I don't quite understand what that should have to do with the future which you claim to have photogr…"

"Oh, come now, Professor, do you still not understand," they all cried at once. "Later on the man took up a career as a journalist, he's purifying the taste of the people and is now art editor with the Pan-German Press."

At that the scholar was so surprised he dropped his cigar and was so amazed he could hardly think of anything to say.

"Hmm, hmm – that however, now that however!"

PRINCE RUPERT'S DROPS

Do you see the pedlar with the tangled beard over there? They call him Tonio. He'll come to our table soon. Buy a little gem from him or a few Prince Rupert's drops; you know, those drops of glass that burst into tiny splinters if you break off the thread-like tail. A toy, nothing more. And look at his face while he's here — his expression!

There's something deeply moving about the way the man looks, isn't there? And what's in his toneless voice when he lists his wares: Prince Rupert's drops, spun women's hair. He never says spun glass, always just women's hair. When we go home I'll tell you the story of his life, not in this dreary inn — out by the lake — in the park.

A story that I would never forget, even if he hadn't been my friend whom you now see as a pedlar who doesn't recognise me anymore.

Yes, yes, can you believe it, he was a good friend of mine, back then when he was still alive, still had his soul, hadn't yet gone mad. Why don't I help him? He's beyond help. Don't you feel that one shouldn't help a soul that having gone blind is feeling its way, in its own mysterious fashion, back into the light — perhaps into a new, brighter light? And it's no more than his soul feeling for memory when Tonio offers Prince Rupert's drops for sale. Let's get away from here now.

Isn't it enchanting, the way the lake is shimmering in the moonlight.

Those reeds — over there by the bank! Dark as night! And the way the shadows of the elms slumber on the surface of the water — in the bay over there!

I often used to sit here on this bench of a summer's night, when the wind went whispering, searching through the rushes and the splashing waves hit the roots of the elm trees, drunk with sleep, and I would think my way down into the soft, secret marvels of the lake, see shining, glittering fish in the depths slowly moving their fins as they dream, old, moss-green stones and dead wood and shimmering shells on white gravel.

Would it not be better to be lying — a dead man — down there on soft mats of swaying weed, having forgotten your wishing and dreaming?

But I was going to tell you about Tonio.

Back then we were all living over there in the town; we called him Tonio even though he actually has a different name.

And you've presumably never heard of the beautiful Mercedes? A Creole woman with red hair and such strange bright eyes. I can no longer remember how she came to the city — and she disappeared a long time ago.

When Tonio and I met her — at a party at the Orchid Club — she was the mistress of a young Russian.

We were sitting on the veranda with the far-off sweet tones of a Spanish song coming out to us.

Garlands of incredibly magnificent tropical orchids were hanging down from the ceiling: *Cattlëya aurea,* the empress of these flowers that never die, odontoglossums and dendrobias on rotten pieces of wood, shining white loelias like butterflies from Paradise. Cascades of deep-blue lycastas — and the thicket of these blossoms, entwined as if in a dance, gave off an intoxicating aroma that always fills me once more when I recall the events of that night that remain in my mind, as sharp and clear as if in a magic mirror before me: Mercedes on a wooden bench, half concealed behind a living curtain of violet vanda orchids, her narrow, passionate face completely hidden in the shadow.

None of us said a word.

It was like a vision from the *Arabian Nights* — I remembered the tale of the Sultan's wife who was a ghoul and crept off to the graveyard when there was a full moon, to eat of the flesh of the dead. And Mercedes' eyes were resting on me as if in assessment.

A vague memory came to me as if once, in the distant past — in a life long, long ago — cold snake's eyes had fixed me with a stare such as I had never been able to forget.

Her head was leaning forward and the fantastic tongues of a Burmese *bulbophyllum* were caught in her hair, as if whispering new, outrageous sins in her ear. Back then I realised that you could give up your soul for a woman like that.

The Russian was lying at her feet. He too said not a word.

The party was also exotic — like the orchids — full of strange surprises. A negro came in through the door curtains offering glittering Prince Rupert's drops in a jasper bowl. I saw Mercedes, with a smile, say something to the Russian, saw him put one of the drops between his lips, keep it there for a while then give it to his mistress.

At that moment there shot out of the darkness of the tangle of leaves a huge orchid, the face of a demon with pendulous, greedy chops — no chin, just shimmering eyes and wide-open, bluish jaws. And this fearsome plant-face was quivering on its stalk, swaying as if with evil laughter — staring at Mercedes' hands. My heart stood still, as if my soul had been looking down into an abyss.

Do you believe that orchids can think? At that moment I felt that they could do so — felt the way a clairvoyant feels, that these fantastic blooms were rejoicing at their mistress. And she, that Creole with her sensuous red lips and hair the colour of dead copper, was an orchid queen. — No, no — orchids aren't flowers — they are satanic creatures. Beings that show us the feelers of their form alone, feigning eyes, lips, tongues for us with sensuously intoxicating swirls of colour, so that we should not have even the slightest idea of the dreadful viper's body which — invisible, and deadly — is concealed in the realm of shades.

Drunk with the overpowering aroma, we finally went back into the hall.

The Russian shouted a farewell to us as we left. It was truly a farewell for death was there behind him — an exploding boiler tore him to pieces the next morning.

Months passed and now Mercedes' lover was his brother

Ivan, an unapproachable, arrogant man who avoided all company. The two of them lived in the villa by the town gate — away from all their acquaintances — just living out their wild, crazy love.

Anyone who had seen them as I did — taking a walk round the park in the twilight, snuggling up together, talking almost in whispers, lost to the world, not even glancing at the world around them — would realise that these two individuals were bound together by an overpowering passion foreign to us. Then — suddenly — Ivan also had had an accident when, in some mysterious way, he fell out of the gondola during an apparently unplanned balloon trip.

We all thought Mercedes would never get over the blow.

A few weeks later — in the spring — she drove past me in her open carriage. Nothing in her placid face suggested she had been through sorrow. I felt as if it was not a living woman that had driven past me but a bronze Egyptian statue, its hands resting on its knees and its eyes fixed on another world.

This feeling even became part of my dreams: the stone statue of Memnon, with his more-than-human calm and empty eyes, driving off into the dawn in a modern carriage, going on farther and farther towards the sun through the purple glow of the surging mist; and the shadows of the wheels and horses, infinitely long — strangely distorted — a greyish violet, twitching over the dew-wet tracks in the early-morning light.

Then I was away on my travels for a long time, seeing the world and many wonderful sights, but few made the same impression on me. There are colours and shapes out of which our soul spins waking, living dreams: the ring of grating in the road under our feet at night, the splash of oars dipping in the water, a wave of fragrance, the sharp profile of a red roof, raindrops falling on our hands — they are often the magic words that wave such images back into our minds. There is a deeply melancholic ring, like the sound of a harp, about such felt memories.

I arrived home to find Tonio installed with Mercedes as the Russian's successor: dazed with love, bound hand and foot, heart and senses — like that other man. I often saw and spoke to Mercedes: the same unbridled love in her. At times I felt her searching look on me.

Tonio and I sometimes met in the apartment of our mutual friend Manuel. And one day he was there sitting at the window — a broken man, his features contorted, like those of someone who was being tortured.

It was a remarkable story he told me in a hasty whisper: Mercedes — a satanist, a witch! Tonio had discovered this from letters and documents he had found in her apartment. And the two Russians had been murdered by her through the magic power of her imagination and with the help of Prince Rupert's drops.

Later on I read the manuscript myself: the victim, it said, is shattered to pieces at the very moment when the Prince Rupert's drop, which he had had in his mouth and then given away in the passion of love, is broken in church while High Mass is being celebrated.

And Ivan and his brother had each come to such a sudden, horrific end!

We could understand Tonio's rigid despair. Even if it were only through chance that the spell had succeeded, what an abyss of daemonic loving there was in that woman! Loving so alien and incomprehensible that we normal people with our understanding sink as if in quicksand when we try to use our concepts to throw light on this terrible enigma of a cancerous soul.

We spent half the night, the three of us, listening to the old clock ticking as it gnawed away at time, and I searched and searched in vain for words of comfort in my mind — in my heart — in my throat, and all the time Tonio's eyes were hanging on my lips: he was waiting for the lie that could benumb his pain.

And when Manuel — behind me — came to a decision and opened his mouth to speak — I knew he had without turning round. Now — now he would say it.

A clearing of the throat, the legs of his chair scraping on the floor, then silence once more for what seemed like an eternity. We could feel it — now the lie was groping its way across the room, uncertainly feeling the wall like a soulless spectre with no head.

Words at last — false words — as if withered: "Perhaps… perhaps… she loves you in a different way from the others."

Deathly silence. We sat there holding our breath: it is just the falsehood that doesn't die — it swithers this way and that on jelly-like feet and is about to fall — just one second to go!

Slowly, slowly Tonio's features started to change: the will-o'-the wisp of hope!

The lie had become flesh!

Should I tell you the end? I dread putting it into words. Let's get up, I've got shivers running down my spine, we've been sitting here on this bench for too long. And the night's so cold.

You see, Fate looks at humans like a snake — there's no escape. Tonio once more sank into a whirlpool of wild passion for Mercedes, he walked at her side, her shadow. With her fiendish passion she kept a tight hold on him, like an octopus down in the depths.

One Good Friday Fate stepped in: early in the morning Tonio was standing outside the church door, bare-headed, clothes torn, fists clenched, trying to stop people going to the service. Mercedes had written to him — and that had driven him mad; in his pocket they found a letter in which she asked him for a Prince Rupert's drop.

And ever since that Good Friday he has been living out the dark night of the soul.

THE QUEEN
AMONG THE BRÆGENS[7]

That gentleman over there is Dr Jorre.

He has a technical office and doesn't associate with anyone.

He regularly has his lunch at one in the State Railways restaurant, and when he comes in the waiter brings him *Politics*.

Dr Jorre always sits down on it, not because he despises it but in order to have it to hand at any given moment, for he reads it on and off while he's eating.

He's a strange person anyway, an automaton who's never in a hurry, never says 'Hello' to anyone and only does what he wants.

No one has ever observed an emotional reaction in him.

---

7 'Brægen' is an Old English word from which 'brain' derives; as 'Bregen' it is apparently still in use in parts of north Germany for animal brains used in cooking.

"I would like to set up a purse factory — it doesn't matter where as long as it's in Austria," a man said to him one day, "I'll spend such and such an amount on it — can you arrange that for me: with machines, workers, sources of materials, distribution and so on and so forth — quite complete, to put it briefly?"

Four weeks later Dr Jorre wrote to the man that the factory buildings were complete — on the border with Hungary; the business was registered with the authorities: twenty-five workers and two foremen taken on from the first of the month, also the sales staff; leather from Budapest and alligator skins from Ohio were on their way. Orders from purchasers in Vienna, at favourable prices were already entered in the accounts. Banking arrangements made in the various capitals.

After deduction of his fee, five florins and sixty-three kreuzers were left from the money he had been given — it was in postage stamps in the left-hand drawer of the desk in the boss' office.

Just the kind of business Dr Jorre did.

He'd been working in this way for ten years now and probably earned a lot of money.

Now he was once more involved in negotiations with an English syndicate and they were to be concluded at eight the next morning. Dr Jorre was to earn half a million from them, his competitors believed.

It would no longer be possible to eliminate him, they thought.

The English thought so too.

And Dr Jorre above all!

"Come to our hotel in time tomorrow," one of the English said.

Dr Jorre gave no reply and went home. The waiter, who had heard the remark, simply smiled.

In Dr Jorre's bedroom there is just the one bed, one chair and a washstand.

Deadly silence throughout the house.

The man is lying there, stretched out and sleeping.

Tomorrow he is to reach the goal of his efforts, having more than he can ever spend. What will he get up to then? What are the desires that stir this heart that beats so cheerlessly? He has presumably never confided that to any person. He is quite alone in the world.

Does nature do something for him, or music, or art? No one knows. It's as if the man were dead — not a breath to be heard.

The bare room is asleep with him — no rustling, nothing. Old rooms like that aren't interested any more.

Thus the night passed — slowly — hour after hour.

Was that not a sob, while sleeping?

Huh, Dr Jorre doesn't sob. Not even in his sleep.

And now a rustling. Something has fallen down, a light object. A withered rose, that was hung on the wall by the bed, is lying on the floor. The thread holding it has torn; it was old and had become rotten. Light on the ceiling of the room — presumably the light of a car from the street.

Dr Jorre rose early. Washed and went into the neighbouring room. Then he sits down at his desk, staring into space.

How old and decrepit he looks today.

Lorries drive past outside; they can be heard rumbling over the cobbles. A plain, dreary morning, still half-dark, as if it would never more dawn with joy.

That people have the courage to live on in such conditions!

What's the point of all that, working morosely in the dull fog.

Jorre is playing with a pencil. The things on his desk are spaced out at regular intervals. Absent-mindedly he taps the paperweight on the desk in front of him. It's a lump of basalt with two greenish-yellow olivine crystals — they're like two eyes staring at him. Why does that disturb him to such an extent? He pushes the lump to one side.

He keeps having to look at it. Who was it that gave him that kind of look, so yellowish green. And that only very recently?

Brægen... brægen...

What kind of word is that?

A dream face is taking shape inside him. Last night he dreamt of the word — yes, just a few hours ago: he had gone into a frosty autumn landscape. Willows with their branches hanging down. The foliage dead on all the bushes. A thick cover of fallen leaves on the ground, dusted with water, as if they were bewailing the sunny days when they had still been up there — in the wind —rejoicing and quivering, those silvery-green children of the willow.

It makes a particularly dreary rustling when your feet brush through the dry leaves.

There is a brown path through tangled bushes grasping at the air like frozen claws. He sees himself going along this path. In front of him an old woman in rags is hobbling along — bent low — with a witch's face. He can hear her stick thumping the ground. Now she stops. In front of her in the dark shadow of the elm trees is a marsh and there are swathes of green over its insidious surface. The witch stretches out her stick; the surface is torn apart — Jorre looks down into the unfathomable depths.

The water is clear, crystal clear, and down below a strange world appears: naked women, writhing like snakes, are moving down there; gleaming bodies are swimming in a swirling dance. And one, with big green eyes, a crown in her hair, looks up at him, waving a sceptre over the others. At that look his heart cries out in woe; he feels his blood taking in those eyes and her green glow starting to go round and round inside him. At that the witch drops her stick and says:

> *"She who once was queen of thy heart*
> *now is queen here among the brægens."*

And as her words die away, thick swathes gather over the marsh.

> *Who once was queen of thy heart...*

Dr Jorre is sitting at his desk with his head on his arm and crying.

The clock strikes eight; he hears it and knows that he should be going out. But he doesn't go. What is the money to him!

His willpower has abandoned him.

"She who once was queen of thy heart, now is queen here among the brægens."

He keeps on going over it in his mind. The spooky autumnal image is there inside him, unmoving — and the green eyes are circulating in his blood.

Whatever can the word brægen mean? He has never heard it in his whole life and doesn't know what it means. It means something horrendous, unutterably sad, something wretched — he senses — and the cheerless clatter of the lorries on the road goes to his sick heart like stinging salt.

THE SLIMY PATCH
IN CARP COVE

One day the numerous members of *Hydrophilus Rowing Club* received a circular from the committee saying that old Korbinian Hugendubel had been found dead, drifting in the Club dinghy on the 'slimy patch' of Carp Cove, and, in accordance with his wish expressed in a document he left behind, his body had been deposited — wrapped in the Club flag as was the established custom — in that part of the lake, to which the authorities had only given permission after initial reluctance. All the Club gentlemen were baffled by this for no one had any idea who Korbinian Hugendubel was. For many long years the ninety-year-old had gone under the nickname of Dr Bompus and looked after the boats, so that his real name, as well as the fact that he had been one of the outstanding male rowers seemed to belong, not just for the others but even for himself, to days long gone.

Why was he generally known as Dr Bompus? Presumably

it was the sailors of the Yacht Club and other types with business on the shores of Lake Starnberg who had given him the name that seemed to mean *bonbon* or sweet: whenever there was a full moon the old man used to spend hours fishing at night in the slimy patch of Carp Cove, oddly enough using sweets as bait, of which he bought great quantities with the generous tips he received. As was well known he never used hooks. He's just a fool, people thought, never understanding his response of, "I'm not that inconsiderate by any means." After days out angling, he was always glowing with contentment and when the young men of the youth section asked him why, he would just mutely give them his enraptured smile or occasionally say. "Mathilda just loves a nibble."

"Presumably he imagines that some female water deity graciously accepts his sweet offerings," one of the Club members said, and when others expressed doubt, especially as since 'Bompus' was exceptionally intelligent and, as a former student of philosophy, extremely well educated, they decided to carry out an experiment to see if he really didn't understand that the sweets quite naturally dissolved in the water of the lake. They covered a few little pebbles in sugar icing and slipped them into his supply of sweet bait, so that they would remain attached to the line when he pulled it out of the water.

The result of this malicious trick was apparently amazing. For a while the man, they said, appeared to be out of his mind and thinking of committing suicide. "Mathilda must be seriously ill, she's not taking the sweets anymore," he'd exclaimed a few times, wringing his hands. — At least that was what was said in the Club. By now it is impossible to be certain whether that was the case. What is a fact is that in the

Hydrophilus Rowing Club logs of seventy years ago there are extensive entries in the hand of Korbinian who at that time was the pride of the Club as a first-class rower in a skiff:

"After almost two years of slaving away in training I succeeded today — a windless day — of reducing my record of 7.29 over 2,000 metres in the skiff to 7.10. The sports reports say that even the famed Canadian Edward Hanlan never had a better time the 7.22. MY temples are throbbing! It means I'm better than him, the most phenomenal rower the world has ever seen! And should I regret having given up everything — my studies, wine, tobacco and even love — for that? Love and all the rest of it, what is that anyway? Nothing more than a hindrance on my way to the world record. There's just one thing that annoys me — or should I not call it superstition but some stupid trick of chance? However precisely I concentrate while training on the position of the oars as I draw them back, however correctly I put the blades in the water so as not to produce any counter-swing and however well I pull through, I can never get the record below 7.25 unless I carry out a decidedly blasphemous action before the course. Perkins — that English ass of a trainer — maintains that if you want to achieve a time that is below what is humanly possible — under 7.22 like Hanlan — you have to chuck a lump of sugar into the water beforehand. Even he has no idea why, but he says he tried it out himself earlier on. After a while, once he'd got married, even the offering of sugar didn't work anymore, from which he concluded that the water sprites or whoever allowed themselves to be bribed with sweeties were not only sweet-toothed but also liable to jealousy. His only response to my objection that it was clear that it was the result of his breaking the vow of chastity and not some metaphysical business of the water sprites was to shrug his shoulders. What should I do now? Should I really chuck a sweet or a piece chocolate into the water before a race? If that should help me win would I not be detracting from my sole fame? No, I'd be like King Günther who was helped to a world-record long-jump by Siegfried in the cloak of invisibility.

One year later there is the following entry in the log book:

"International Regatta on July 15… Skiff: first Emil Piefke, Sport Rowing Club, Berlin: 7.24; second by a whisper: Korbinian Hugendubel: 7.25. Hugendubel, initially well in the lead, suddenly drops behind. It's as if the progress of his boat is being held back by an invisible hand for his work with the oars continues to be excellent." There is a scribble about this in Korbinian's handwriting: ('Oh God, if only I'd thrown a sweet in the water!')

He raced against a professional rower and thus lost his amateur status and, back in Bavaria, took employment looking after the Hydrophilus Club's boats. And it was then that his strange habit of attaching sweets to an angling line and 'fishing' with it at night in Carp Cove began. Certain occasional notes that he made in his private logbook reveal (as the Club Secretary established after the old man's death) the event in Hugendubel's life that led to this remarkable mental derangement. It says there:

"So it gave me no peace and I wanted to see if it was possible to improve on the time of 7.10 I'd achieved in Henley. It was midday and blazing hot and I rowed out to Carp Cove, that part of the lake sheltered from the wind which made it ideal for training. This time I threw three particularly nice sweets into the water and, when the hand of my stopwatch was on 'one' I set off at breakneck speed. I could already feel I would reach a speed I'd never achieved before but then my skiff gave such a jolt that I fell off the sliding seat. However I didn't capsize for I'd kept a tight hold on the sculls. I expected the boat to be filled with water at any moment, for I thought I'd struck a large log of wood, that would naturally splinter the bow of my skiff. But nothing like that happened. As I later established, the front third of the boat was covered in a kind of slime. Perhaps I'd brushed against or struck a huge fish — something like a whale? I just couldn't get out of my mind why, since time immemorial, that part of the lake had been popularly known as the 'Slimy Patch'."

At this point the report in Hugendubel's logbook breaks off and it was only through the efforts of the Club secretary, Herr Dr K. Paungarten, a psychoanalyst by profession, that a final fragment in the old man's handwriting was found. It says:

"How often have I made the stupid joke myself: What is imagination? Answer: You put on a herring's tail, get into a tub of rainwater and imagine you're the fair Melusina. Even today I'm still thoroughly ashamed of that. But how could I imagine, even in a dream, that fair Melusinas really do exist — and in Lake Starnberg at that! I still had sunstroke from that memorable row in the blazing midday sun and such a headache and dizziness I could hardly keep myself in the skiff, but I rowed on, this time at quite a slow pace, When I looked round, I saw such an incredibly beautiful naked girl sitting astride the bow of my boat that I was totally overcome…

It is only today that I know what love is!… Keep on going for world records? What's the point? My existence has finally found its goal. Oh Mathilda! This very day I will present to the committee of Hydrophilus a request to be appointed Club servant. Then I will be able to spend my time with Mathilda undisturbed, enjoying the secret sweet happiness of being seen as a fool by those blind folk while knowing more, a thousand times more, and enjoying bliss a thousand times more profound than them, the poor, wretched creatures…"

"What we have here is a case of psychological complexes," said Dr K. Paungarten, after he'd once more read out this extract from Hugendubel's notes one Sunday afternoon in the clubhouse. "It is of great interest to the specialist and opens up far-reaching perspectives in the area of psychoanalysis. The unheard-of self-constraint to which the unfortunate man subjects himself, going to the very limit of irrationality to break his own world records, and then the absurd, uncompromising decision, to suppress all impulses instead of reacting to them was naturally bound to lead to collapse and overcompensation — I hope I am putting this in a way that is sufficiently comprehensible for the layman — that we can see here. The most disturbing hallucinations were bound to occur. All that proves that Hugendubel…"

"Nonsense! Team line up!" The interruption came from the rowing coach. "Meier, wind in the motorboat, we'll go out along with the racing eight onto the practice course. The good doctor can keep blethering on here."

A few days later an amusing note appeared in the water sports sections of the newspapers:

Clearly Frogspawn
During a recent training outing in the eight of the

Hydrophilus Rowing Club, accompanied by the motor boat of the trainer, Piefke Junior (the grandson of the famous skuller of the *Sport* rowing club in Berlin) both boats, travelling at top speed on the so-called slimy patch in Carp Cove suddenly hit an invisible obstruction so violently that some of the team were thrown head over heels into the water. Since neither of the two boats were at all damaged and, moreover, had large amounts of a glutinous substance on the bow, they provide a solution to the reason why that part of our lake is called the Slimy Patch… clearly there are times when large masses of frogspawn appear there.

Postscript: Some nasty person had written a message in pencil on the copy of the newspaper that was delivered to Dr K. Paungarten:

Until now slimy excretions have never been found in the waters of the lake but solely in the brains of psychoanalysts.

THE ASTROLOGER

July, the Bavarian month of ice, had arrived.

Profound darkness. I was lying in bed and couldn't sleep. Out in the park the old trees were creaking in the storm and, since they belonged to our neighbour and blocked my view during the day, I fervently hoped they would get blown down. Lumps of ice were hammering the windowpanes: 'hail' is what it's popularly called. Someone was whistling and howling, rattling the doors — that could only be the bride of the wind! "So, what does she want from me, I'm an old gentleman already," I muttered, turning onto my other side. "The hussy ought to get married and settle down, then there'd be an end to all this nonsense," I said grumpily, going to sleep a moment later.

"Can you hear that rumble of thunder?" I woke with a start — did I say that for no good reason, just dreamt it, or is it the ghosts of dead poets murmuring round me with their pointless questions.

Before I could solve that problem a clap of thunder blared

out its crackblastboom — only much louder than I would ever manage to write down — making the walls quiver and I instinctively and incautiously shouted, "Come in."

There! The room door opened quietly — bewildered and quivering with horror, lips bloodless, I stammered — half as a man of letters, half as a devout Christian — "Ancestress, Grandmother, mother and child, Jesus, Mary and Joseph!" But it had no effect, the door opened even wider.

"It'll just be my dachshund, Isidor Palmleaf," I thought, trying to persuade myself (I call him that because he has wonderful fan-shaped hands and big, dark Jewish eyes) and I listened, full of confidence, hoping to hear a scratchy gallop across the smoothly waxed parquet floor. — A vain hope. No scratching!

I was about to cover my face with the blanket, in order to make any ghosts that might have got in think I wasn't there at all, when I saw by the usual pale gleam of a flash of lightning that there was already a ghost in the middle of the room. Pulling myself together quickly I took refuge in Goethe plus Coué and thus, denying everything that was present, declaimed to my subconscious: 'That's a trail of mist, my son,' but the spectre remained, raised its right hand in warning and put a triple master's diadem on its forehead and a similar sceptre in its hand shining.

To my immense relief I now recognised him: it was Demetrius Hasenknopf, the world-famous astrologer who, not long ago, had been unable to resist casting my horoscope. Or, to be more precise: it was his astral body.

"He wants to warn me, the good fellow," I sensed, with trust trickling through me, "of something terrible in the near future. But what could that be? And what did the diadem and the ruler's mace mean? I sat up and searched for a polite cliché, for I assumed it was the spirit of one departed that I had before me but by then he had already transformed himself into my valet Corbinian and announced, "Sir's tae cum to't telephone, there's an urgent dispatch frae Munich."

What? In the middle of the night? And what if the lightning should hit me on the ear?! But I dashed out of the room, scurried down to the phone to hear, my hair on end, the alarming news:

"Message posted Munich, midnight. Mars — Mercury — Sun have entered into quadrature. Uranus in decline. Terrible catastrophes for Europe in the immediate future. Athens is the only safe place still remaining. Advise immediate flight there. Hasenknopf."

The receiver slipped out of my quivering hand. Hasenknopf is Germany's greatest astrologer! If he should send a telegram like that can there be any hesitation?! It is well known that astrology is the sole reliable science nowadays. Moreover, the weather forecast in yesterday's newspaper said: Improvement will go on. Oh yes, now I understood: 'will go on' its way, perhaps never to return! — "Corbinian! Pack the suitcases!" And as if taken by some dark inspiration, I added, "and don't forget the latest neo-classical literature! Who knows, I might need it in Athens."

I sat there shivering, waiting for morning to come. Mustered a few old friends. Plane. Vienna! No use. Trieste! Quick get the Xenophon out; what is it he puts so well? Of course: Thalatta, Thalatta! The sea! The sea! A steam galley puts out to sea. Forging ahead. What's that approaching? A line of black? Jews? No, Corfu! We hold our breath. Kaiser Wilhelm's *penteconter* comes into sight. But the bold captain has the valves weighed down and heats the boiler with ham. Ha! The way this noble ship is flying along on its keel! Hurrah! we've got past! A Netherlandish prayer of thanks: the disaster has mercifully slipped past. And now, blasted misfortune! What's all this? Didn't Hasenknopf say that the sole safe place was Athens! And right now here of all places, *nebbich!* a revolution's broken out!? Martial figures with drooping moustaches, ballet skirts and buckled shoes are marching with thunderous steps along Kephisia Street to the Castle, counting out loud as they do so: *"Ena dyó, ena dyó"* so none of them tread on another's heels.

I had been careless enough to make myself known as a poet and as punishment I was dragged off to the Acropolis. Weeks of torment. Day and night I was guarded and threatened with cudgels and hexameters by seven hoplites armed to the gills. Fortunately for me, years ago they had learnt German in a prisoner-of-war camp in Görlitz — which now proved their undoing for, cunningly, I got them to read the works of Paul Ernst, which my dear Corbinian had packed in my suitcase — and they immediately fell asleep. Thus, I managed to escape. True, I was stark naked, for all my clothes had been stolen, but since I was holding my arm out in front of me with a wet towel over it, they let me through everywhere — in the belief that I was filming the Apollo Belvedere.

Disguised as a crate of grapes I mingled with the throng of hydridiots and, Odysseus-like, escaped by ship to Syracuse, where, being completely rotten, I was auctioned to the highest bidder among the vinegar dealers. Do not ask, gentle reader, what I had to go through on the way when the grapes started to ferment!

With the proceeds of the auction, I bought myself a bullwhip — secretly thinking of the astrologer Hasenknopf. "But oh," I said, "will I ever see him again?" The quadrature of Mars, Mercury and the Sun — how could it be that Europe was still standing!? The stars do not lie. Or do they? And the Italians I asked about it didn't know where it is. I had no hope of ever finding it again, even though I was beside myself with amazement that the Italian boot was undamaged. I am sure, I said to myself, that northern Europe will have been razed to the ground by all kinds of whirlwinds. Tattered and torn I headed off home, weary at heart, barefoot along the Apennines on the endless Via Latrina.

Months had passed and only then was I happy to have Rosenheim, that notorious Bavarian junction, behind me, but there was still absolutely no sign of the destruction I had imagined. — "Of course, Hasenknopf will object that Bavaria, especially Upper Bavaria, could not really be counted as part of Europe," I told myself as I strode along, but I still took an even fiercer grip on my bullwhip, murmuring "Hasenknopf!" to myself right down to the heels of my shoes whenever my feet started to get weary. I arrived in Munich towards sunset one Saturday. There were large posters on every street corner; "Hasenknopf lecture today — German League of Astrologers 'Hosenknopf'[8] (a misprint, of course) — Prof. Hasenknopf's prophecies have been becoming literally true for months (my bullwhip twitched like a divining rod) the astrological law of causality fully effective in Bavaria — New

8 Hasenknopf = Harebutton; Hosenknopf = Trouserbutton

catastrophes imminent!"

In the grip of a wild fury and with a spring in my step I hurried off to the place where the meeting was being held only to run into Ho-no: Ha-senknopf, the Chairman of the League of Astrologers right at the entrance.

"Oh, back from Athens, are we?" he said, glancing at my well-travelled feet. "You were truly fortunate not to be here during the quadrature of Mars, Mercury and the Sun. I'm well aware," he added in appeasing tones, when he caught sight of the glint in my eyes, "that you have always had your doubts about the reliability of our science, but now, when everything has turn-ed out to be quite literally true — I mean back then in July…"

"Ju… then?" I stuttered, greatly astonished.

"Well," Mr. President explained, "hardly had you flown off to Athens than the remarkable agitation broke out in the Bavarian Parliament and the price of beer was raised by 3.7 pfennigs. I ask you, is there a more striking proof that everything can be read in the stars?!" he was going to continue speaking but we were torn apart by a throng of astrological maenads from the Prussian north. One of them — called the 'Sirius Tart' by the malicious — stuck a leaflet in my hand before skipping off on her sandals into the hall, at the top of which Hasenknopf was already climbing up onto the podium, his van Dyck beard stuck out in front of him like a goat's (clearly in allusion to the sign of the zodiac).

The place was too packed for me to get close to him, so I just had to content myself with a crack of my bullwhip.

A lay person in astrology, with no clue about the more

profound interrelations of earthly matters, would in this case probably have sung with the poet, "It was not meant to be," but after a short period of impotent fury I said to myself, "Clearly, they — the bullwhip and Hasenknopf — have been born under quite different planets, otherwise it would definitely have come to a conjunction between them by now.

Resigned, I set off for home in Starnberg, but the half-hour journey was to become the source of unheard-of revelations for me. Apparently, my ascendant, Jupiter, must be in an extremely favourable position, otherwise I could hardly enjoy its blessing to such an extent. What I read on the train — by the light of my petrol lighter for, as is well known, after the onset of darkness the lights in the carriages are switched off — in the pamphlet that had been wished on me made me realise — late but in this case soon enough — what deep ethical value there is in astrology and its use in practical life. It said there in black and white and brazen word that instinct was merely a contemptible leftover from the animal kingdom and that to adhere to it was a crying shame for an upright person. For example: to eat, drink, digest on impulse — how contemptible when one can work out with a pencil from the position of the planets the precise second when one or other of them is to happen without, as now, running the danger of confusing or even combining one function with another!

Hasenknopf, O thou blessed translator of the heavenly science, only now do I know what the meaning of the above-mentioned vision of you with the threefold diadem and the sceptre in your hand was: you or the likes of you will become the much longed-for Führer of the German people and, with the happy removal of all instinct, will lead them up to the light. *Heil* Walter Scott!"[9]

---

9 A pun on: *Das walte Gott* — 'Amen to that' or 'I hope to God it will happen'. It sounds like a warning about Hitler whom Meyrink, as Hartmut Binder says "fled in April 1933 and went back to Prague" (in: *Gustav Meyrink: Ein Leben im Bann der Magie*, Vitallis 2009.)

DER MAGIER GUSTAV MEYRINK
(THE MAGICIAN GUSTAV MEYRINK)

an extract from the article by the journalist Kemil Oraj
(pseudonym of Jaro Limek)
published in *Neues Wiener Journal*
on 3rd June 1934

During a holiday from the war, I met Gustav Meyrink in Munich. With *The Golem* he had just hit the longed-for jackpot which for him meant the end of many financial problems. At that point he was looking for a place in Starnberg and not long afterwards bought the nice property on the lake. In the years after the war we often sat together there, spending hours in stimulating conversation, the most amusing of which being those that dealt with occultism, mysticism, magic and suchlike. As is well known, Meyrink was very much occupied with these matters. He was very well read about them and they were an inexhaustible source of ideas and stories; he was also in contact with all kinds of magicians, dervishes and yogis, often in far-off places such as Arabia, India and China. With visible pleasure he liked to call himself a conjurer, or even more a 'magus'. According to what he said, he quite often did magic, though with a character like that you could never be really sure whether to take him seriously or not... however I did several time observe very strange things happening around him and had experienced things through him that have no straight-forward explanation. Meyrink's property was a short distance from Starnberg, on the road to Possenhofen. The villa, 'The House by the Last Lamp' as he called it, was pretty close to the side of the lake, only separated from it by a narrow flower bed. On the side of the house facing the lake was a veranda with wide windows, where the author most liked to sit. From there you had a really splendid view out over the lake to the east and south and, when the weather was fine, of part of the Alps, which made a splendid backdrop to the Starnberg panorama.

Unfortunately, however, a huge tree on the neighbouring property blocked the western part of the mountain range, so that the Karwendel Hills and the Zugspitze could not be seen,

So, he had approached the owners of the neighbouring villa with the request that the tree be felled. We were all surprised when they simply refused his request. Meyrink was annoyed but didn't give in. At his request friends became involved, offering the neighbours a considerable sum for the removal of the tree or at least the lopping of the large branches on the side by the lake. But this attempted intervention was in vain. They refused to make even the slightest change because this tree had been planted on a special occasion by some of their ancestors and was therefore sacred to the neighbours.

From that moment on Meyrink couldn't rest, the tree spoilt almost the whole property for him, he could hardly work anymore but worked on a plan, eventually telling us he would remove the tree *by magic.* From then on, contrary to his habit, he frequently went to Munich and studied certain old books of magic both there and at home.

That went on for a few weeks until one day he was cheerful and in a good mood again, spending time on his beloved place on the veranda. We thought he had finally overcome his irritation and anger, so we strictly avoided mentioning the oak tree again. He it was who brought the subject up, telling us he'd arranged a great magic spell: he had buried something in the ground, as he told us, the great annoyance would be gone by the next new moon. We just smiled...

But, lo and behold, precisely at the time mentioned there was a great storm, there were several lightning strikes in the area and one hit Meyrink's notorious tree! Unfortunately, the lightning caused hardly any damage: a few twigs had fallen off and there was an ugly black mark on the trunk, apart from which there was nothing we could see when we went to look at it the next day. Meyrink had mixed feelings about all this: on the one hand he was proud that at least something had happened, on the other hand disappointed at the lack of success of his spell. But he still wasn't giving up. On the contrary: he started going to Munich again, immersing himself in his books, and once again there came a day when he told us the matter was settled and this time for good. Now, however, he refused to give us any more details, however much we plied him with questions.

For a long time after that there was no mention of the oak tree and I at least had completely forgotten it until one morning some weeks later when I had a telephone call from a mutual friend asking me to go at once to the House by the Last

Lamp: overnight the tree had vanished without trace. At first, I thought it was a joke but that was wrong. The oak tree had actually disappeared and Meyrink was beaming all over his face. The gardeners and inhabitants of the neighbouring villas were standing round the spot where the oak tree had been, people had come down from the main road, even a policeman was already there. What we saw was strange: the tree had been sawn off a foot and a half above the ground, there were a few splinters and some sawdust lying around and yet was there was no trace at all of the rest of the wood, of which there would certainly have been a great amount. nor of all the leaves and twigs — yet less than fourteen hours previously we had all seen the huge oak tree in its usual place and those who knew about such things said that it would have taken even a dozen workers at least three days to clear the ground so completely.

The neighbouring family, furious at the theft, in particular because it was their favourite tree that had been stolen, initiated an investigation, the result of which was as follows: during the previous night the few people who had passed the site had seen a man with a lantern at work with something close to the tree; they had been surprised but not thought anything more about it. Workers who had been on their way into the town that morning had also noticed a man, who was a complete stranger, leading a horse-drawn cart laden with wood out of the property. But however hard they searched for the man and the cart, they had vanished, leaving no more trace than the oak tree had, and they were never found again…"

Even stranger is my memory of another experience that I alone had with Meyrink. In 1923 I had to travel to the Middle East on business. When Meyrink heard that he asked me to do him a favour, should I get to Baghdad. In Kasimen, close to the old town of the Caliphs, there was, he told me, a *sayyid*, a descendant of the Prophet, a very holy man with whom he had an occult relationship. He wanted to send him some documents, the contents of which were very important, and I had to keep their presence absolutely secret. I was particularly happy to promise all this because I hoped that through the *sayyid* I might meet some very interesting people, members of famous orders of dervishes, of which there were a large number in that area. My only problem was that I had no idea at all of when I would be travelling through Mesopotamia. He, however, comforted me, telling me that for the moment time was irrelevant, he just absolutely wanted some person to take the documents — the post was far too unreliable and the documents too important. He gave me the name of the holy man but did not have a precise address, however, he was sure that it would be easy to find that by asking in Baghdad. Then he gave me a well-filled envelope, with five-fold seals but otherwise nothing written on it.

I set out on my journey. Unexpectedly business dealings meant I lost almost six months in Russia and was sent from there on to Persia, where I was compelled to stay for several months more. During that time, I kept the little package, together with my own important papers in my locked suitcase and was in the habit of checking on them once a month. During one such check in the summer of 1924 I was horrified to find that the envelope had gone and even the most thorough search failed to find it, while nothing at all of my own things was missing. Extremely irritated and greatly embarrassed I did everything that was humanly possible to get back the envelope that had been entrusted to me — suspecting the servants and bringing in the police, even though such a theft by the staff is something exceptional in Persia. But all in vain so, embarrassing as it was the next time post for Europe was being sent, I would have to write to Meyrink and confess the loss. However, before that happened, I was told that an old man, a very great saint as the valet put it, had been waiting for me for hours and refused to be turned away. I immediately had him let in and the person who appeared was a magnificent old man with a long beard, in Arab dress and a huge white turban. After the usual local greetings, he apologised for not having come to see me the previous day; he had been looking for me in the capital, however, and had only heard quite late on that I was spending the summer in the mountains. He was bringing me greetings from his friend, the *sayyid* from Kasimen, who had heard that I had been looking for the package from Mussye Merung — that was how he pronounced the name. This, as was quite right, had come into the possession of the *sayyid*, and they were extremely sorry that, by an oversight, I was being informed of this too late, causing me unnecessary concern. And he went on to say that there had been no theft at all, my suitcase was still completely untouched. Since, however, the document had suddenly been urgently needed in Bagdad and the postal service from Tehran would take at least twelve days, his revered and venerable friend had been compelled to procure it quickly in a special way. And he begged me once more for forgiveness.

I was totally baffled. For even if I believed there had been a theft, it was totally incomprehensible how my visitor could associate the name of Meyrink with the package and how he could speak of the *sayyid*. I had definitely not mentioned it to anyone since I left Starnberg — even in the embassy I had specifically avoided mentioning a name. I was never given an explanation and the old man in the turban refused to allow me to interrogate him. I immediately wrote to Meyrink, telling him in detail about the astonishing encounter. When, five weeks later, I was back in Europe, I made a great effort to get an explanation out of him as to the nature of my little adventure. But he didn't say anything, just gave a mischievous little smile, and calmed my fears by telling me that his envelope had come into the hands of the *sayyid* at the right moment, about which he had been informed ages ago…

Books by and about Gustav Meyrink which are available from Dedalus

The five novels translated by Mike Mitchell:

The Golem
The Angel of the West Window
The Green Face
Walpurgisnacht
The White Domican

A two-volume collection of short stories. *Volume I (The Opal and other stories)* translated by Maurice Raraty and *Volume II (The Master and other stories)* translated by Mike Mitchell.

A sampler for Gustav Meyrink's complete works edited and translated by Mike Mitchell:

The Dedalus Meyrink Reader

The first English language biography of Gustav Meyrink written by Mike Mitchell:

Vivo: The Life of Gustav Meyrink

The Golem – Gustav Meyrink

'A superbly atmospheric story set in the old Prague ghetto featuring the Golem, a kind of rabbinical Frankenstein's monster, which manifests every 33 years in a room without a door. Stranger still, it seems to have the same face as the narrator. Made into a film in 1920, this extraordinary book combines the uncanny psychology of doppelganger stories with expressionism and more than a little melodrama... Meyrink's old Prague – like Dickens' London – is one of the great creations of city writing, an eerie, claustrophobic and fantastical underworld where anything can happen.'

Phil Baker in *The Sunday Times*

'Gustav Meyrink uses this legend in a dream-like setting on the Other Side of the Mirror and he has invested it with a horror so palpable that it has remained in my memory all these years.'   Jorge Luis Borges

'A remarkable work of horror, half-way between *Dr Jekyll and Mr Hyde* and *Frankenstein*.'   *The Observer*

£8.99   ISBN 978 1 910213 67 4   280p   B. Format

The Green Face – Gustav Meyrink

'Of the volumes available to the English public, *The Green Face*, first published in 1916, is the most enjoyable. In an Amsterdam that very much resembles the Prague of *The Golem*, a stranger, Hauberisser, enters by chance a magician's shop. The name on the shop, he believes, is Chidher Green; inside, among several strange customers, he hears an old man, who says his name is Green, explain that, like the Wandering Jew, he has been on earth "ever since the moon has been circling the heaven". When Hauberisser catches sight of the old man's face, it makes him sick with horror. The face haunts him. The rest of the novel chronicles Hauberisser's quest for the elusive and horrible old man.'

Alberto Manguel in *The Observer*

'Gustav Meyrink's most mystical novel yet. First published in 1916 to critical and commercial acclaim, the book is set in the near future of post-war Amsterdam, and is an elating vision of apocalypse. A trait of Meyrink's novels, particularly *The Green Face*, is its depth of meanings, which go beyond one single interpretation. It deals with love, a galaxy of grotesque characters, but it has other hidden significances, like the mystic conception of life. Full of symbols and parables, it's a very complex novel that is difficult to understand, but certainly worth the trouble.' *Buzz Magazine*

£9.99   ISBN 978 1 910213 89 6   224p   B. Format

Walpurgisnacht – Gustav Meyrink

Comic and fantastic, gruesome and grotesque, *Walpurgisnacht* uses Prague as the setting for a clash between German officialdom immured in the ancient castle above the Moldau, and a Czech revolution seething in the city below. History, myth and political reality merge in an apocalyptic climax as the rebels, urged on by a drum covered in human skin, storm the castle to crown a poor violinist 'Emperor of the World' in St Vitus' Cathedral.

'It is 1917. Europe is torn apart by war, Russia in the grip of revolution, the Austro-Hungarian Empire on the brink of collapse. It is Walpurgisnacht, springtime pagan festival of unbridled desire. In this volcanic atmosphere, in a Prague of splendour and decay, the rabble prepare to storm the hilltop castle, and Dr Thaddaeus Halberd, once the court physician, mourns his lost youth. Phantasmagorical prose, energetically translated, marvellously evokes past and present, personal and political, a devastated world.'   *The Times*

£9.99   ISBN 978 1 907650 17 8   165p   B. Format